PRAISE FOR
SHATTERING **GLASS**

"With *Shattering Glass*, Connor Coyne has fashioned a hypnotic tale that is at once universal and otherworldly, with writing that is as inventive as the plot."

– GORDON YOUNG
Author of *Teardown: Memoir of a Vanishing City*

"Don't be fooled by the playful tone and pastiche of Connor Coyne's second novel. *Shattering Glass* presents serious questions of identity and morality, posed by vivid characters of a strange and violent world."

– JEFFERY RENARD ALLEN
Author of *Rails Under My Back* and *Song of the Shank*

"It's the First Year Experience from Hell, yet in often gorgeous and startlingly original prose, Connor Coyne gets at something heartwrenching and heartwarming about coming of age in academia."

– JAN WORTH-NELSON
Author of *Night Blind*

PRAISE FOR
HUNGRY RATS

"In confident, purposeful, evocative prose, Connor Coyne places you in a family where no one is watching out for you, and you had better watch your back."

– LEILA SALES
Author of *This Song Will Save Your Life*

"Connor Coyne has created a richly imagined world full of surprises for his strange and wonderful characters. This work is wickedly funny and sinfully dark. I found myself both delighted and repulsed, often at the same time!"

–ARLENE MALINOWSKI
Author of *What Does the Sun Sound Like?* and *Aiming for Sainthood*

ATLAS

Short Stories by
Connor Coyne

MORE BY CONNOR COYNE

Hungry Rats, a novel
Shattering Glass, a novel

CONNORCOYNE.COM
HUNGRY-RATS.COM
GOTHICFUNKPRESS.COM

ATLAS

Short Stories by
Connor Coyne

GOTHIC
FUNK
PRESS

GOTHIC FUNK PRESS
www.gothicfunkpress.com
Flint, Michigan

ATLAS: SHORT STORIES BY CONNOR COYNE
Copyright © 2015 by Connor Coyne
All rights reserved.

Designed and Illustrated by **Sam Perkins-Harbin**
forge22.com

ISBN-10: 0989920224

ISBN-13: 978-0-9899202-2-3

10 9 8 7 6 5 4 3 2 1
First Edition

To the Atlas Coney Island.

3833 Corunna Road
Flint, Michigan

24-7-365ish

TABLE OF CONTENTS

FAREWELL, MY LOVELY

An essay, originally published on connorcoyne.com
(24 July 2014)

On the occasion of your funeral, I find myself reminiscing about our fling together. We never saw each other seriously. It was more of a one-night stand. I, myself, was more of an Atlas and Grapevine kind of guy, but I still cherish our time together.

It all happened one boiling summer night in '98. I was nineteen. At 3 AM I went out to cool off by sitting with some other kids I didn't know on the ventilation grate outside Bower Theater. That was the last summer the city felt so alive at such an hour, not only because the scorch tormented all of us without air-conditioning, but also because men and women carried their signs back and forth on the picket line all night long down on Bristol Road and up on Dort Highway. In the summer of '98, Flint was a city that never slept.

My stomach was making all sorts of loud noises, so I asked two of the kids where they thought I should go to get a bite to eat. They didn't think I should settle for fast-food fries; didn't I have any self-respect? They encouraged my colonial aspirations, and sent me off to meet you at chivalrous Knight on Corunna. I'd seen you before, but I'd never really noticed you looking at cars as if from a high window, looking out at hungry nite owls all across the West Side. You had that tender smile, those narrowed eyes, that welcomed, that forgave. I recognized your conviction that humans are fallible because humans are hungry, so you would forgive us and feed us. After all, there is plenty of pain in this world, and all of our life is just one long goodbye.

I playback the elation I felt when I saw you that night. I recall your perfect sense of balance, one leg before the other, a tentative confidence, no fear of falling, but only of stumbling. In your poise, you held a tray with a tasty coney island carved out of beef heart and ground up Koegels, rough and dry and red like granite, onions so fresh and wet they sparkled like diamonds, mustard of pure sunshine, the bun firm but damp with steam, so delicious, a real Flint Original. Famous like the sun that rained down on San Juan at the bottom of the bay. Famous like the desert sand dusting Poodle Springs condos. Famous like the pinprick spark lights of Coney Island that leaped out at tired Macedonians across the relentless gray waves of the North Atlantic. "Welcome to the U.S."

When they disembarked, your Uncle Bob and your Aunt Kewpee bought train tickets to Flint, and there they stirred up a dry sauce that made mouths water from Seattle to Miami and hearts flutter from Boston to San Diego. Your ancestors had seen Lady Liberty, but when you were born, you became the Lady in the Lake State. Your parents had presided over the rise and you saw the decline. You watched that diminishment with compassion and understanding. You fed us for thirty years. Thank you for feeding us.

Now they have taken you away and another one of the greats has fallen. Most of your brothers and sisters died long ago, but some few continue to look out toward green lights with grace under pressure, waiting for years that will answer questions from this "callus on the palm." The Atlas, the Starlite, the Capitol, the City Diner, the Olympic, the Golden Gate, Angelo's, Tom Z's, Tom's, and Star Brothers. We pray and order and tip so that they will escape your tragic fate.

What is your consolation?

I offer this: As you settle into the big sleep, remember that you fed us and we are grateful.

We are grateful and we will remember.

ORBITUARY

Originally published in Moomers Journal of Moomers Studies 5
(December 2013)

CHAPTER 2017

Zeugma Olan didn't give two fucks what his friends or family thought about his project, owing no doubt to that time when his wealth excused a crime, not through the subtle efforts of needy magistrates or weak judges, but simply through the naked exercise of filthy, filthy lucre. He had murdered a man in a bar and in the crudest of ways. Smashed a bottle over the man's head, then a chair, then strangled him bare-knuckled, then garroted him with balloon ribbons for good measure. But Zeugma was a billionaire, and now, decades later, he was building a prison.

The prison was a giant hollow sphere a thousand feet across. Zeugma was to be suspended in the center of the thing, which would then be cast into orbit around the Earth at some hundreds of miles up. Inside, at the center of the space, it would be dark, milquetoast warm, and silent. Zeugma wouldn't have anything to grab onto, no matter how he flailed, so he would be move in orbit around and around. Skeptical observers thought Zeugma was reading too much Kafka too literally, but they didn't understand. See, he was the one to escape painful sensation. Everyone else was the prisoner. The inside of the sphere was freedom. Everything on the outside was misery and entrapment.

Of course, it didn't go according to plan.

The sphere fell into the ocean instead of being shot into space.

It fell down, two plus miles, but Zeugma, in the silence and darkness inside the cell reified his patience. As far as he was concerned, he was entering a land of diminishing pressure, and so he dreamed an ersatz orbit up from the Atlantic currents and discovered his cherished ennui down in the depths.

CHAPTER 2027

When Zeugma's pod fell into the ocean, Daphne's sins all caught up with her and turned her into water, and she started to roll downhill. It took a very long time, as "downhill" doesn't mean much in Chicago, but ultimately she came to rest at the bottom of a tenement-style building on Hyde Park Blvd. just south of 55th Street.

Her sins boiled down to this: When she was sexually frustrated she felt lonely, and when she got lonely she became mean. So there was the time when she spit on the bus driver's face and of course he had done nothing wrong (it wasn't his fault that bus was forty minutes late – in the rain – in thirty degrees – and Daphne didn't have an umbrella – and nobody would share theirs – and she had woken up that morning in a cold apartment because nobody would spend the night and wake her up with French Toast sizzling in the kitchen, coffee black and bitter in the carafe, and for that matter no friends to visit, no family (because she was too mean and obtuse), but it wasn't the bus driver's fault that the magnetic strip on her card was wiped and so she had to walk all the way home). That was the sort of sin that gets you turned into water.

A thirsty cat came down to the basement and lapped Daphne up.

CHAPTER 2029

When Z hit the ocean floor the earth's polarity rotated ninety degrees, earthquakes went out all over, and for some reason the sun flared like a flashlight in a toddler's hand. Daphne was trickling through the cat. She slowly possessed it.

Upstairs, dishes were being washed against a primary color backdrop. It is a crime that more neighborhoods aren't painted bright and bold like La Boca in Buenos Aires. It doesn't dismiss serenity. Serenity and zen enunciate a vocabulary of vibrancy.

Just like progressive moms and dads so noisily boast that their daughters are happy tomboys and murmur that their sons occasionally play with dolls, it isn't quite the meaningful equivalence they suspect. The stereotype of femininity is reticence and submission, and the stereotype of masculinity is ambition and individuality. It is a kind of chauvinism, then, that even in our progressive efforts we give deference to ambition and individuality. The world could use more reticence and even, occasionally, more submission (listen listen listen!). But don't listen to me: I've surely been brainwashed.

CHAPTER 2039

What kind of a douche wears gloves to keep his hands warm but then strolls around shirtless outside?

Even after the earthquakes, the distant mountains rose up at steep-angled inclines, sharp rays aimed at the sky. Humans saw the mountains as sacred places, but even moreso the sea and the sky. Their arcs. Their planes. Their empty vast evenness. So more than half of America rolled down into the large valley between her sides. The largest room in her house. The walls of languid mountains had mythology but population is denied. She ate an apple pie or a peach. It was always unseasonably warm or cold. Jay and Sky, Kyle and Erin and Divine, Cora and Mephit and Shine: They all sat out on the porch wearing Mardi Gras masks even though it was six weeks into Lent. Drinking too-cheap beer and marveling at that coiled darkness. Everyone knew but nobody cried about what Simon was doing in the bathroom. It was sad and a bit gross. So of course they all sighed.

CHAPTER 2053

One gray morning Mephit and Erin found Simon sitting dead on the can, having expired and exhaled in pursuit of momentary erotic exhilaration, and the power strip around his neck had prevented any short-circuity mischief, but this was a Gothic story so nothing ought to be amiss.

They called the authorities, of course, but while they were waiting for the arrival they were starving, so Mephit cut off Simon's head and Erin seasoned and boiled it. When the head was bubbling and tender, they scraped the cheeks off with stale tortilla chips. Simon tasted delicious. The first visions his friends saw were horrific rusted skulls spinning and leering and promising all kinds of strangulation in stifling darkness – a small space, no doubt, but you sensed it, you couldn't see it, you couldn't see shit, no walls around you, no floor beneath, no ceiling above – but soon transmorphed into something less awful: Squamous snapdragons blossomed all over, and when they pinched the petals a dulcet xylophone chime sounded, and they drank lovely honeymead, and swam down beaches of ruby-colored sand, and generally resigned themselves to an immortality of laconic euphoria.

CHAPTER 2063

Pachelbel's Canon sucks, sez every cellist ever. But gellists are, for the most part, okay with it.

When Zeugma struck the ocean floor, the trans-magnetic impactμ-rotation caused the earth to start orbiting along a line of longitude. The effect was profound. If humanity was to survive (doubtful, doubtful) it would have to gather along the twilight border that slanted lightly into and away from the sun, but even here the climate was bizarre and extreme. Half of the Earth baked. The other half froze. On the cold side cold the night skies were startling and pure, while on the hot side hot the sun exhibited the majesty of a dancing demon. Both hemispheres became hazing destinations, for rites of initiation, inductions, and grotesque ceremonies. Chicago was in the blessed zone. It had a damn chance!

Once, before he did himself in, Simon was dating a girl who just wanted to wake up to eggs and French toast, strong coffee and maple syrup. He was scared of her edge though. He was pretty weak and wussy himself. He took off before she woke up.

CHAPTER 2069

The sun moved.

Daphne stretched out on the ottoman and opened her eyes wide. Most people thought her feline eyes – cones of this and that – could only see in black-and-white, but this wasn't true. Just like an old computer monitor she didn't know that her color palette was limited. All she knew was that she saw colors colors and these colors are funky.

Dammit, the sun wasn't on the ottoman anymore, and the ottoman was absolutely the best. The hardwood floor wasn't that uncomfortable but it wasn't ideal, either.

Oh, but as luck had it, with the Earth's altered orbit, time had dragged the sun across a shoebox, which was almost as good as the ottoman. Daphne leapt into the box. She'd felt utterly comfortable after all. Loneliness had never felt quite so delicious.

She thought she smelled mouse.

Mouse would be absolutely delicious.

CHAPTER 2081

We're all going to die.

Watching Lake Michigan sunrise off of the Point.

Toni Morrison has written powerfully of the liminal status of the Great Lakes having more than a shore but less than a coast. Truly, those of us who are honest have to admit (and it isn't a matter of beauty, but rather of sublimity) that there is a tangible / spiritual / palpable difference between any lake and the Great Ocean. The ocean rises up from the horizon like a mother and wraps her All around you. If you're like me, you somehow inherited cankers, and whenever you get stressed out they erupt within your mouth. The salty ocean with all its bigness causes a searing pain with the sores but it draws the pain away, draws the pain away, draws the pain away, on purple waves, receding endlessly toward orange sunsets and distant dun-colored clouds, as far away as forever, and god knows, you might even find a trajectory you can follow forever without having to deal with land. No way you can pull that off with a lake.

And Jay is grateful for his football scholarship, which has kept him from the East Coast, which is now plunged into the darkness of endless death.

CHAPTER 2083

So this one time I went on a road trip to Emporia, Kansas.

Missouri was pretty forgettable, since I was going at night.

The Speed Limit was 70 MPH, so that was nice.

The birds will rescue us, but the octopodes are divine.

Alas, the broletariat is alienated from the means of seduction.

CHAPTER 2087

We're all going to die.

That's what Shine shouted when he looked out the windows of the heavily fortified tenement and saw the jawa-gimlet-eyed minions of hellish Zeugma staring in like Stygian stars, and stalking like lumbering bugbears up Chicago's prime-numbered streets. Safe on 55th and 57th, but 53rd, 59th, beware. The time had ripened for Molotov cocktails and fertilizer bombs, and so the cadre readied their chainsaws and axes and hatchets. Ripened for the not old but the no longer young – we aren't spring chickens anymore, kids! – to make a final stand, to go out in a literal blaze of glory (though but figuratively, as Chicago has already been established to lie in the life-sustaining twilight zone) and so the flashlight eyed creatures hopped out more innocent-like than they really are – their true nature – diabolism – and they started destroying us, and prose can never capture the violence of murder and the hideousness of soul-cannibalism, but the balm is that it all ends in calm, which can be rent with words. Jay and Sky and Kyle and Erin and Divine and Cora and Mephit and even wise old Shine were all sleeping now. They slept. They never woke up. It no longer mattered whether their demise had been grotesque. It was. It was. They weren't anymore. And that's a-okay.

CHAPTER 2089

So Carl Sagan and Rumi sat in a cave and played the Game of Life, and they made various and contrary statements about the significance of human action, except did they really contradict one another?

Carl had bad gas from too many chickpeas, but Rumi was a very good sport about it.

CHAPTER 2099

End nigh, hour late, there was an almost violent temptation to simply phone it in. But this isn't that kind of postmodern tripe and anyway, now our phones are cognitive extensions and – hell! – Calico sez it's a big, bold step toward eventual immortality. So nobody ain't phoning nothing in.

Simon favored Bombay Sapphire. He never got to travel much, but the blue glass, filtering compact fluorescent light through benthic shades of serenity evoked the dimming of sub-something kelp forests, and was about as close as he would ever get.

He always liked pounding more booze than was healthy for him, and that, doubtless, had some role in his happenstance self-murder mere moments before his friends died like mayflies several minutes past their sell by-date.

CHAPTER 2111

Self-loathing was far too strong an expression, but there's this house where I used to live and I'd drive past it from time-to-time to see how it was doing. First time, it looked pretty much the same as it had when I lived there – a broad and deep porch, chipped, worn, well-loved, and a gorgeously feeble tree casting cooling shadows through its autumn years. Then I drove by later and saw that the grass had all been torn out. The front yard was mud and straw, but I stopped to say "hi" to the family that lived there – to see how they liked living in the house where I had lived – and they seemed nice enough. Then I came by a few years later and the place was all abandoned and boarded up. No one lived there. No one was going to live there. Then I came by a couple years later and the place was gone. The dappled tree was gone too. Its autumn had passed. Its winter had arrived. We all died.

Zeugma killed everyone with his downward plunge, except himself. He stayed alive a long time in his metal sphere, impatient after all and always imagining his fast orbit around the world, his catharsis, his perdition, a soft sharp scent of ozone. He didn't know that he was the very last human alive on the whole earth.

Try to remember what the pollen was like, though.

It was worth smelling.

It is still worth remembering.

CHAPTER 2113

... the wire ... follow the wire ... because ... we are all going to die a very fuchsia death ... cats ... Daphne always followed the sun ... nine lives ... the wire ... follow the wire ... because ... a fuchsia death ain't so bad ... death ... dead ... cats ... and don't forget ... that Daphne ... always ... yeah, Daphne followed the sun.

IMMORTALITY

At the end of the day, it is always best to consult the incontrovertible. You don't need to be a brain surgeon to know that there are more hurricanes in Kansas than in Alaska. It isn't rocket science to say that scissors cut easily through air. And everyone knows that travels downstream will take you into the world while the mountains, the hermitage, and meditation all lie up the river. Great cities ride on the oceans' shores. Great solitudes perch on lonely peaks.

This last observation was the incontrovertible thing that spoke to Stan on the day they finally shut down the line at Buick City. As a young man living in a shake-side house, with a postage stamp yard, well-mowed, he had smelled the silent screams of cut grass. That ragged, sharp summer-scent that made him almost go crazy thinking about places warm year-round, about round lanterns glowing, and about the beautiful women – dark hair and dangerous dark eyes – that danced in their glow. That was his dreaming youth.

His middle-age wasn't turning out quite as hot as he had hoped. As another summer wound down, the smoke stopped rising from the power plant off Leith Street and the demolitions began for real. Stan couldn't stand life in his dying factory town any more, but neither could he contemplate the heady heat of the ultimate downstream: river and lake and river and lake and the St. Lawrence. Stan knew that the seaway didn't open into the tropics, but it was all hot as far as he was concerned. Port cities. Warehouses and mixed-up people. Mixing freights. Halifax routes might lead as far south as Rio de Janeiro or São Paulo. Stan couldn't take it. Not in his present tiredness and half-assed sadness.

Stan couldn't go downstream, and he wouldn't stay where he was. That left just one option: he'd have to head upstream. Into the interior of his Self and Solitude. Into the mountains? Hardly. The wooded uplands of Lapeer and Tuscola Counties were as close as he was likely to get to local aloneness. He set out on his way.

"What's your purpose?" she asked him.

"My what?" he answered.

"Where you goin'?"

"Upstream. To get away from everyone."

She snorted at him. She understood the absurdity of his plan. He was an idiot. Slow. Clueless. Unwilling to change. But she saw herself as agile and changing and, therefore, beautiful. She flitted among the branches and looked down on him with an ill-defined expression. Probably contempt or affection.

"Who are you?" Stan asked.

"I am the Sylph," she answered, and shook rain from the branches over his head.

Stan saw another incontrovertible: that each season embodies an era of one's life, with spring as youth, summer maturity, autumn decline, and winter death. Stan wasn't dying yet, but he definitely felt the slope of decline.

Similarly, Richfield Park, where Stan and the Sylph stood in the shadows of the cathedral oaks, breathed an air of longstanding autumn. The park, not far from the city, saw the changing of the seasons. Rough and ragged undergrowth choked its wild corners. Over all, however, towered the master oaks. Once the dying brown leaves littered the forest floor, they'd lay there for years, slowly decomposing. Thick shadows choked out the sun, even at the height of the summer solstice, and so the aspect of the park was always dim, dimming, dimmer.

"Maybe I'll stay here," Stan said. "It's just like fall. And I'm just like fall."

The Sylph dropped her contempt. They must be married. A destiny had been fulfilled. She was spring and had always looked for a spirit, mortal or fae, that could correspond to her, which she might oppose and define, and (as the crunchy hippies say) make a yin for her yang, a sweet to her sour, a honey to her vinegar, a mild autumn to her vicious spring. The Sylph had felt partial to her immortal kin: the atomies, brownies, and pixies, but nobody had ever fit the bill. Stan did. Like misshapen puzzle pieces that fit cleanly together, they had been made for each other. They lay together, and nine weeks later the Sylph gave birth to two children. Twins. A boy and a girl. Alexander and Ariel.

Alexander, sun bright, sharp eyes, forceful and quick, easily angered but quick to forgive, made friends easily. He laughed and made jokes and was rough and everyone liked him. Ariel, moon cool, careful and cautious, worried about saying the right thing, about listening closely, and so she perceived more and understood the world better than anyone else. Both children filled their parents with love, but still, this was a broken family. Mortals and Immortals might speak the same language but their souls do not understand each other, and the children were caught in-between. They belonged in neither the forest nor the factory town. They belonged nowhere. So Ariel grew up with her mother in Richfield Park, living in the quiet glades between the thick trees, while Alexander moved in with his father in Kearsley, and went to school there, and played football, and made the honor roll. The twins knew their parents' freaky story, but they didn't understand where they were going in their lives, or why. Supermortal. Subimmortal. In the abundance of potential it was difficult for them to see where their reality might lie.

Then, on the eve of the childrens' eighteenth birthday, when Ariel would sprout her wings and gain the ability to turn invisible, and Alexander would receive his scholarship to go to college in L.A., their parents took them out for breakfast at Gillie's Coney Island, to sit down over pancakes and coffee and tell them the truth about their future.

The twins listened closely.

They were, they thought, ready.

"Jeezus," said Stan, taking a long pull at his coffee. "Why the fuck we ditch Leyland? He would'a won us the series someday. He always fuckin' did. Where did our patience go?"

The Sylph took a drink of her water. "You two have grown up in an upstream place: you have grown up looking inward. You two have grown up in an autumnal place. Both the park and the city are filled with the signs of dying. But you are not locked inward, nor are you dying. You are young, and being young, your final identity is not yet determined. You will not get the chance to decide what you want to be: nobody knows the answer to that while they have the power to affect its outcome. You will, however, get to decide how and where you will seek out the answer. Will you stay with autumn or will you seek out another season? Will you continue the path upstream, to interiors, or will you go down and out into the mainstream currents of the world?"

The twins answered at the same time.

"Spring!" declared Alexander. "Downstream!"

"Autumn," murmured Ariel. "Upstream."

"I'm not surprised!" said Stan. "Well, your future is longer than mine. How about some bacon to go with your eggs?"

"But there is more," said the Sylph. "Your bodies both contain opposite principles. They are divided against themselves, and as a result you are dying, just as your father is dying. But: If you find a way to become everything – to imagine everything, experience everything – then you will be immortal, just as I am immortal. If you do not do this, then you will grow old and die just as all humans must."

"I will go out into the world and experience everything," said Alexander. "I won't die."

"I will travel inward and imagine everything," said Ariel. "I will not die."

"If you say so," said the Sylph.

The waitress brought the bacon.

* * * * *

Within a month of this conversation, the twins lost their parents forever. Stan had a bad heart and one day he pushed himself too far, mowing the lawn through the August heat. A week after Stan's death, the Sylph drifted away. As an immortal, she could not die, but she was still made out the air, and so a strong wind dispersed her and her children never saw her again.

Still, the twins had been anticipating this moment for years. When they found themselves alone, they packed their bags, Alexander loudly hopeful, Ariel quietly hopeful, and set off in search of immortality.

* * * * *

Ariel packed a small bag of walnuts and greens, a small pillow and blanket, and followed the Flint River northeast from the park that had been her home for eighteen years. As she climbed upstream the Flint River filled the massive basin of the Holloway Reservoir, and the factory lights of the city behind her faded to a misty carbon sheen. She bought some more nuts in Columbiaville, watched the fish splashing in the water beneath the big bridge, and continued deeper into the wild. By the time she found a virgin copse, midway between the villages of Mayville and Clifford, the leaves were falling again. There, in the middle of the grove, she discovered an ancient hickory tree with a hole about halfway up. Ariel climbed the tree, squeezed herself into the hole, and made her way further and further up the inside of the trunk. Near the top, she found another opening, this time out onto the sky. She couldn't see, from this vantage, precisely what the season was. Neither leaves nor branches occluded her view. The hole angled northward, away from the sun, so she could not judge the season from the angle of light or the length of the day. She snuggled warm in her sleeping bag, ate her nuts, and trained herself to ignore the passage of time through smell, sound, touch, and taste. Eventually, the sleeping bag and pillow, too, dissolved and she felt herself becoming embedded into the rich pulp of the hickory. She looked up, daylong. She drew deeper and deeper into her interior. She saw only the sky: sometimes blue, sometimes black, and sometimes gray. One day, that, too, went away.

* * * * *

On the day of the Sylph's departure, Alexander headed off in the opposite direction of his sister. He followed the river downstream, into the city with its weed-infested brownfields and neighborhoods of wood-framed rotted porches and pitted ghetto palms. On a single, shiny spit of pavement downtown – the favored sector – he managed to hitch a ride with a grizzled old man who drove him as far as Saginaw, the next city downstream. Saginaw was smaller than Flint, but its river was larger, and so Alexander was able to book passage on a small boat that took further downstream to Bay City. There, he caught passage on another ship – a freight ship – and this took him through the Saginaw Bay into Lake Huron, and from there down the St. Clair River and Lake and on down the Detroit River. To Alexander's left sprawled the bright gardens and condos of Windsor, while the mirrored windows of the Renaissance Center reflected each other in mutual congratulation.

The ship moved on into Lake Erie, bypassed Niagara Falls on its way into Lake Ontario, and made its way up the St. Lawrence Seaway: Kingston, Montreal, Quebec City. Once the Atlantic had been breached, the ship made land at Halifax, and Alexander waited a week, enjoying the brisk and salty air on Citadel Hill and the pine shade out at Point Pleasant Park. He eventually boarded another ship southbound, and yes, he did dock at Rio de Janeiro and the São Paulo. A third ship carried him around Cape Horn and back into the tropics before docking at Salinas, Ecuador. After Alexander spent a month on hammocks on the beach, a fourth ship brought him the rest of the way north to Los Angeles. It had taken him a year to go around the continent this way, and he was hungry for discipline, so he started his classes at Loyola Marymount. He worked hard and spent winter weekends letting a wind as mild as Michigan Mays kiss his brow. It was a dry, desert wind, but in time, he learned to touch it carefully enough to catch a faint lick of salt, the ocean, the world beyond with all of its teeming multitudes.

Alexander had learned that these were not simply multitudes of humans. There were birds, too, and beasts and insects. Plants and diatoms and protozoa and bacteria. The multitudes of living things, trillions of them, all bleeding their way through his experience and trying to survive or propagate. To be fruitful and multiply. His eyes got wet sometimes, it was so fucking magnificent in the sunset.

Alexander's life did not stand still. Every time he stayed up too late or drank too much or danced too long, played too much football or baked out on the beach at high noon on a summer day, and the weariness, a fatal fatigue of inertia, started to weigh his eyelids shut, Alexander remembered what the Sylph had told him about immortality. He drank another cup of coffee and did jumping jacks. For the most part, it worked. He spent most of his time awake and working hard.

One evening, he met a girl in Echo Park and they shared tamales and Italian ices. He took her out for pastry and then they walked down to the ocean on Venice Beach. The sun rose behind the Santa Ana Mountains and the bodybuilders and Rollerbladers and surfers came out to do their work in the salt breeze, and Alexander got down on one knee and proposed to the girl. Her name was Sarah.

A year later Alexander got his degree and then went on to earn another degree and his certification in civil engineering. Sarah worked as a lawyer for civil rights cases. Both Alexander and Sarah enjoyed successful careers. They made a lot of money, but they also did work to be proud of. Their lives felt full and fuller, and then fuller still, when Sarah gave birth to a baby boy. More children followed: girls and boys. They moved south to Orange County and into a small house with a white marble balcony that offered a view of the ocean blue, a mile, half-mile to the west. The house was warm and dry with a faint citrus scent floating in from nearby orange orchards, but Alexander was most obsessed by the circular motif spanning their balcony. It was a concrete balcony, rectangular, with a single gate opening onto some stairs down, but the balcony wall comprised a grid of concrete circles, suspended with concrete crosspieces. The ocean blue bled through each circle, unchanging day by day, heavily shadowed, and it gave Alexander more comfort than anything else in the world. They imparted a stillness to his fast-beating heart, while he tapped his foot and dwelt anxiously on what he had achieved and what he had not yet accomplished.

Still, an anxiety settled deep into his chest, like a rock. Like he had swallowed a rock in Kearsley or in Richfield Park long ago. He couldn't digest it. It sat there. It wasn't going anywhere. The rock: How could Alexander achieve immortality and keep everything that he cherished in life? His career, his home, his wife and children? How could he keep any of them? They would fade and pass away. Would he pass away? Would he, like his immortal mother, be dispersed and scattered by a casual wind? Would he forget his name? He knew his past, but would he remember his future?

Time passed.

Alexander started to fear.

Always mindful of that circular grid, he doubled down on his work, engineering pipes, tunnels, ventilation systems, interior spaces with high-tech fans, sleek and spinning blue, without speck or blemish, and silent. Structures that helped interior spaces breathe. That opened them up to the outside air.

"Why are you so worried?" Sarah asked. "Why are you so thirsty?"

Not content with his geometric solutions, Alexander bought a motorcycle and took long rides. He rode on his own, and then he bought a bike for Sarah and they went for rides together. Sometimes they rode as far north as the Bay and then farther still. As far as the technicolor green slopes of the Cascades where white gulls set off against the sea breeze. These were the happiest days of Alexander's life, not because he had solved the riddle of immortality, but because he knew that he was dabbling in the right ingredients: shapes, breathing, motion, and love. His life was worth fighting for. Maybe immortality would turn momentary happiness into permanent joy.

But then, at 3 AM – always at 3 AM – when the afterimage of bright light and the afterglow of phosphorescent desire bled into the pillow beneath him, and his arm fell over Sarah's waist – her breathing belly – he knew that he was going to fail. Success was not possible. Some have obtained immortality, perhaps, but who has ever obtained eternal happiness?

Nobody.

It is impossible on this earth.

When Alexander turned forty, his hair started to gray on the sides, and he took this to be a symptom of his lack of faith.

When he turned fifty, he was diagnosed with diabetes.

When he turned sixty, he started to forget things.

His office closed. Sarah died. Alexander's children went off to start their own careers. Now he knew he was running out of time. He said goodbye to everything and everyone he knew and set out in search of immortality again.

He spent the next twenty years in a fever dream of questions and riddles. His travels carried him all over the world, from the Transantarctic Mountains to the tundra of Siberia, from Galapagos to Madagascar. Alexander traveled everywhere, experiencing everything he could find, learning all he could, and every time he met someone, he would fix his eyes on theirs, look at them deeply and intently and pose the question: Do you have the answer? Will you give me immortality so that I will not die as my father died?

One day, he received an answer.

An old woman milking a goat in the Caucasus mountains somewhere near the border of Russia and Georgia (he did not know on what side) nodded her hardened, cataracted eyes in Alexander's direction and said, "you would like to live forever?"

"It is all that I want!" said Alexander.

"You will find a Soviet sealed capsule at the bottom of the deep Pacific trench. There, at the bottom, past the maze, you will find your answer."

The next year was a flurry of activity, and while Alexander was over eighty now – wracked with pains and mental lapses – he felt a quick burst of his youthful energy return. He was ready his last mortal adventure. His very first immortal adventure.

The ship set out in stormy seas and arrived at the brink of the Marianas. The submersible descended through gray and dimmer gray and dark blue and then mile after mile of blackness, to finally arrive at the deepest point of the deepest ocean on earth. There, they found the Soviet capsule, embedded in the soft ocean crust at a sharp angle. They docked to the airlock and Alexander put on his oxygen mask. He said goodbye to his crew and left the submersible. On the other side of the airlock, the capsule seemed stale and untouched. Absolutely tidy and unspoiled. Nobody was here, nor were there any provisions that might rot. The capsule was bubble shaped, with a metal wheel that unsealed a round door that opened into second, identical capsule. Even though he could read Russian, Alexander couldn't make sense of the Cyrillic script that lined the doors of the capsules. They didn't seem to form real words or sentences, but boiled down a nested and intertwining sets of acronyms and bureaucratic agencies, all existing relative to one another, accountable to nothing or nobody, relevant to each other in indecipherable ways.

Each capsule led directly into the next. Alexander soon realized that he was not under the ocean anymore, because the chain of capsules had entered the earth itself. He wondered about the rocks around the lab, how deep he had gone, and how soon he would start to feel the mantle's heat bleeding through the reinforced skin of the capsules.

As Alexander went deeper and deeper, the Cyrillic script became interspersed with that of a new language, something he had never seen before. It looked like a child's scribbles in its consistency and artfulness, and yet the scrawl seemed systematic. There were repetitive graphemes, swirls that functioned as punctuation, and the occasional interjection of enlarged hieroglyphics.

Alexander realized he had have passed through dozens of capsules.

He realized that he must have passed through hundreds.

He kept expecting to feel the heat of surrounding earth, but he did not.

Instead, the air grew, if anything, more humid. A pungent, organic scent began to trickle through his breathing filter, and Alexander realized that, though it didn't smell rotten or decayed, he was near something else that was living.

Alexander couldn't have told when his position in space changed, but at some point during this journey, or more likely, gradually, through many points, the angle of his expedition shifted. He was no long moving down into the earth. His path had started to slope upward. The capsules no longer displayed markings in any language. The walls had become black and rough. He knew he must be nearing the end because the tunnels had grown narrower and narrower.

At long last, after hours, or maybe even days, of climbing, he opened a final hatch and found himself in tight, narrow space, a tunnel more than a capsule, almost vertical. He put his hands on the walls to pull himself up and was surprised to find that these were made out of wood, caked with with fertile soil. His arms throbbing with pain and exhaustion, Alexander lifted himself higher and higher still. And higher still. With each effort, he moved closer to his goal, though he didn't know what it would look or feel like. He felt that there was a light up ahead. He couldn't see its source. It grew brighter as he moved upward, a vague, atmospheric glow that seeped in among these enclosing woody pores.

Alexander lifted himself up again and again and again, and then, when he was so tired that he thought he might collapse, he finally emerged into the light.

He took a look around.

Up above him, the tunnel narrowed until it was maybe just a foot across. There, it terminated with a hole that opened onto the sky. In that sky, dark blue with night, cool with the ascent of spring or the decline of autumn, hung a beautiful, radiant, pale full moon. All around him, Alexander felt the hollowed out shell of an ancient hickory. To his side, the patient and unchanging gaze of a human skull, gently nested, cradled even, in the soft pulp of the living tree.

WHITE SWAN

You felt your stomach start to go when we breached the polar low.

"What?" I asked. "What is wrong?" You blanched, your face bleached like the plains and ice and snow that rolled away across the Antarctic landscape.

"I didn't expect it to be so windy," you said. And "I didn't expect it to be windy so quickly," Adam said. Overhead, the low groans, ghosts walking their Cirrus tightropes, spun from the ranges. In four days Emily will venture forth from the McMurdo Station (77°51′S 166°40′E) into the glacial ridges and ranges the climb dry beyond. Standing in the polar low. There is a swirling; it moves like cream vanilla. A girl addicted to fast-food soft-serve flavors stands out in the drive-thru asking strangers for change. Perhaps downtown she could be persuasive, but here, out past the city limits the bored commuters take one look at that pink-and-white winter coat, that banana colored hair tied up carelessly; they know she only wants an ice cream. So she pouts and waits. Once her brother got free ice cream by pretending to be retarded, but he's at home right now. She's been waiting for her friends, but they don't come. The sun sets. It's been warm all day, the snow drifts melting into plush cushions and damp marshmallows that finally leak and flood the streets. She starts to walk home.

Walking out under the stars one is astonished how clear they are. One is astonished by the circumference of the light, the diameter of darkness. That's not a figure of speech; it works exactly like that. Emily wends her way up among the jagged glaciers, their encrusted deposits freed up now, fed out, dropped from and among after many thousands of years. The jagged path runs through the glacier, a place where the runoff of melting ice feeds into a crevasse. Over several years, the contact of warm water on ice has widened the black partition considerably; a diameter. But because the path is jagged, because it winds, sometimes cutting off at sharp angles and at others, twisting off to the left like a convection current, there is no place she can turn without seeing the rising walls of white ice; a circumference. It stands like a dark spot on the inside of a cracked egg. It looks out.

At least there will be stars.

"Will I make it to Antarctica?" you ask.

"Will we make it to Antarctica?" I'll ask.

Four days ago you wound your way out from the McMurdo Station and clambered into the glaciers like a salmon slipping upstream. You were there to study sediment; the tiny bits of rocks and stone that got swept up in a vanilla swirl of ice millions of years ago only to be set free now. You study melting and the release rate; the wrinkles that mark the resignation of this old ice, puckering up and dripping away the hundreds of tiny, wilted lines. I was there to study to study to steady the polar low.

Emily has finally gotten her ice cream. At least she will have stars. No matter what admixtures, what extremities of light and darkness one must submit to here below, there always seems the perfect balance up above. Stars do not threaten to crowd or overwhelm, but when we look we always see more.

Adam has gotten his ice cream. He will head home now. He did and he arrived, sneaking in through the side door and creeping up the stairs to his room. He threw away the cone and crawled into bed. He is unnoticed. His nose is running; he sniffs loudly, a snort, and his mother knows he's awake. "Eddie!" she shouted. "Sleep now." "Antarctica?" he whispers and will whisper.

He tried to sleep. The fact is that there are many discomforts associated with this kind of cold. I sat up. I will not be able to shower for many weeks; the water would draw away moisture from my skin. Likewise I must wear heavy wool at all times to trap sweat until I cool and reabsorb it into my body. Back at McMurdo, after six months in the glaciers, I will smell like salted herring, and if I'm not careful, I might lose my hair from the rapid drying out and itching. You too. But we can't smell ourselves.

Still, the Original thinks, if we are here than we might as well see what we came out to see. The ice cream is worth the sticky hands that hold the sheets and comforter. Emily looks out the window at the last bits of melting snow. She realizes that she likes the shape of soft-serve more than the taste. She likes the cyclonic swirl. "Will we make it to Antarctica?" "Will we make it to hurricanes?" "Will we have ice cream?"

If only there were hurricanes where it got so cold out.

Above, in a vast wall that rises from the glaciers like aurora australis, and then like massive vanilla-shaded bedsheets. You squeezed my hand, puffing. "Get used to the cold and the wind," we say. You're rung in, and it rises high and starts to move across the plane. Then the monster starts to move and the wind picks up. Ice shards fleck and spit moving slowly out from the interior. Us. Specks in the eye of a great white swan.

FLINT'S ILLEGAL OCCUPATION

Originally published in Flint Broadside, #18 (2011)

"The State may mould local institutions according to its views of policy or expediency; but local government is a matter of absolute right, and the State cannot take it away."
– Thomas Cooley, Chief Justice of the Michigan Supreme Court

"Early in life I had learned that if you want something, you had better make some noise."
– Malcolm X

Wake the fuck up Flint, Michigan!

You are subject to an illegal occupation. No, not those campers on the corner of MLK and 2nd Ave., but the vampire-office of the Emergency Manager (EM) sitting in City Hall. Now I know, I hear you, life is hard, your back is broken, and the world doesn't care about you, your friends, your family, your children. And you've lost your house, your food, your job, and your dignity. But Malcolm X also said that "when people are sad, they don't do anything. They just cry over their condition. But when they get angry, they bring about a change."

Thesis #1: If you were wondering when to get angry, it was years ago. It's long past time. They have taken so much and now they've taken away your vote, and they're going to keep taking and taking and –

Thesis #2: This isn't about whether Dayne Walling is a good mayor or whether Michael Brown is a good man, or even about whether Flint can balance its budget. It's about democracy. In a democracy, when there's a problem the people fix it. In a constitutional republic like the U.S. the people fix problems by means of their elected officials. The EM is an unconstitutional position. Seriously: Poverty deprives you of the right to self-governance? What sane argument can support such an illogical breach of ethics? Certainly no argument coming from the home state of Thomas Cooley, our nation's most legendary champion of home rule.

Thesis #3: No EM or EFM has ever "fixed" a budgetary crisis. Rather, EM's balance the books in the extreme short term by slashing services and (now) breaching union contracts. This leads to lower standards-of-living and property values, which corresponds to less revenue for the city; a recipe for future budget shortfalls. Benton Harbor's EM has asked that city's policemen to fight fires. Detroit's EM-managed public schools are up to 60 students per class. Pontiac's last EM actually requested the city to be disincorporated.

Thesis #4: None of this should surprise you because the EMs aren't about fiscal solvency or saving cities. After all, what's solvent about cutting revenue sharing for manufacturing towns in the midst of a deep recession? We've got a Republican governor and the state legislature is almost two-thirds Republican. Who elects Democrats in Michigan? The poor. Minorities. Cities. The expedience of EMs with power and incentive to fire elected Democrats is obvious. But don't get outraged on behalf of a political party.

Thesis #5: Get outraged because you've been robbed of your vote. And you aren't being robbed in spite of being poor, minorities, cities... you're being robbed because you are poor, minorities, cities.

"Well," says Snyder, "we try to avoid a financial manager whenever we can –"

Shut up, Rick! This isn't your article. Or your newspaper. Or your city. You don't get to decide.

"How can you thank a man for giving you what's already yours? How then can you thank him for giving you only part of what is yours?"
– Malcolm X

Flint, my friend, it's time to show some self-respect and shut this shit down.

"Stand, you've been sitting much too long, there's a permanent crease in your right or wrong."
– Sly and the Family Stone

"Declare independence, don't let them do this to you!"
– Björk

"We've had the vision, now let's have some fun."
– MGMT

You can...

...rescind the Treaty of Detroit, returning sovereignty of Flint to the Chippewa Nation. We'll even go along with a casino this time.

...collect 365 letters from Flintstones who've suffered decades of poverty and neglect; inscribe the letters onto the Hammerburg Rock with black paint and beautiful calligraphy. Display a different letter each day. Rinse and repeat until the EM leaves.

...occupy City Hall. We have more of a right to be there than any EM.

...ask our elected leaders by what authority they have ceded their office to the state's discretion: Counting Walling, they outnumber Snyder 10 to 1.

...send our elected leaders tangible evidence of cojones: beach balls, truck nuts, and rocky mountain oysters.

...there are hundreds of great protest songs and hundreds of prolific Flint musicians. Add one to each column by recording a brilliant piece of music and sending it viral online.

...demand that today it's your turn to be King of Flint.

...seed the parks and golf courses with apple trees, pear trees, corn, beans, broccoli, peas. You're hungry! If the EM can overturn ordinances at whim, why can't you?

...cripple Lansing with Michigan FOIA requests pertaining to all actions of the government, however miniscule. Sue the state over the tiniest breach and funnel your winnings directly back into the city.

...respond to cuts in public safety with a couple hundred Chevys on the lawn at City Hall blasting Grand Funk and Stevie Wonder unendingly. Don't go anywhere until the EM changes his mind, because we can't be having none of that.

...perfect fusion powered electricity generation. That ought to set us for awhile, but don't slack off on patent registration.

...dedicate 2 hours a week to volunteering for community service; this empowers Flint and increases its capacity to resist intervention. Here's a good one: tinyurl.com/northendsoup

...dedicate 10% of your income (or whatever you can manage) to charity. Here's a good one: tinyurl.com/flintfoodbank

...occupy Genesee Towers. Take a page from Venezuela: tinyurl.com/flintiscaracas

...serenade the EM with vuvuzelas.

...for one night, reappropriate I-69 for all the Blues clubs that were demolished when the expressway went in decades ago. Do the same with 475 for the restaurants that went under with the St. John St. Neighborhood.

...paint our brownfields green.

...for that matter, incorporate the brownfields as a separate municipality. Who is going to come and evict you?

...shut down at least one major street every day.

...are you for real about this? Then take a couple shots of something strong (or even just a couple deep breaths) and take in a foster child: tinyurl.com/questionstoanswer

...however you feel about Michael Moore, he's put forward some fine ideas here: tinyurl.com/mooreofthis

...arrange for a student exchange with other EM-managed cities; guest students can offer suggestions that have worked for their communities.

...get 100 friends. Chain yourselves to the doors of city hall. Repeat weekly. Given the number of police, it'll be hours before the EM can get to his office... then he'll realize we need more police (to cut the chains) and hire 50 or 60 cops.

...send your utility bills to:

Governor Rick Snyder
P.O. Box 30013
Lansing, Michigan 48909
(517) 335-7858

...fax pictures of your butt to:

Governor Rick Snyder
(517) 335-6863

(Make sure to write "Love, Flint" on your butt before sending.)

...what would Jurgis Rudkus say about all of this?

...pool the resources of many people and buy up all the properties on a couple city blocks. If they are anchored by a major road, such as Pierson or Franklin, you would have zoning for business and residential. You could dramatically impact activity in these areas for the better.

...out-Mardi Gras New Orleans on February 21st.

...get involved with the Sugar Law Center, which is fighting the EM law through the courts: tinyurl.com/judicialjustice

...get involved with Michigan Forward, which is fighting the EM law through public referendum: tinyurl.com/popularjustice

...make a common law exception to any EM decree that violates your personal belief; the legal precedent being that the EM -- an unelected citizen -- has such powers, therefore you do too.

...if the U.S. sends aid to nations like Pakistan who shelter terrorists, then surely they'll send even more aid to Flint when you egg all of the windows at City Hall.

...how much of this is Don Williamson's fault? Write him a polite but strongly worded letter. Then shout it through a megaphone from the sidewalk in front of his house (but no trespassing; that would be rude).

...form a committee to draft an amended city charter extremely favorable to the state's wishes. Then shred it because, hey, your opinions don't matter.

...don't get foreclosed upon and evicted. You sit down and stay put. Get legal consultation. If the police do, in fact, arrive, you might suggest that they arrest the bankers foreclosing your property.

...retrieve scrap stolen from the City of Flint from area junk yards to make a brand new water pipeline. If Lake Huron is unavailable, we can just use Rick Snyder's swimming pools.

...open a factory. Create an obscene number of jobs, giving Flint the wherewithal to balance its budget.

...unending block parties, especially this winter.

...1) go here for inspiration: tinyurl.com/newyorkgraffiti, 2) then get Flint on this list: tinyurl.com/flintgraffiti

... or 1) go here for inspiration: tinyurl.com/sweetondetroit, 2) then apply here: tinyurl.com/brutalflint, 3) or here: tinyurl/brashflint, 4) or here: tinyurl.com/beautifulflint. (If you do #4, however, make sure not to damage the building, since students will be coming back someday.)

...occupy the Flint jail and refuse to leave until you've received a hot shower, a warm meal, and a good night's sleep safe from arson and gunfire.

...do you hear the people sing? Perform a public rendition of the musical *Les Misèrables* or, better yet, a literal performance of Hugo's 513,000-word novel, with real barricades and revolutionaries.

...bring Batman to Flint. Gotham City doesn't need him like we need him.

...amass as many votive candles as you can and leave them lit throughout the city, anywhere that seems empty or hopeless.

...first, use all the scrap and detritus left over from the industrial era to build the world's largest particle accelerator. Then use this to produce a high energy density burst far in excess of an exaelectron volt. This will penetrate the potential barrier and trigger a vacuum metastability event. That'll show them!

...convene a shadow government, with its own city council, mayor, and city hall. Observe their governance meticulously.

...hold neighborhood meetings in parks, garages, off the sidewalk, wherever, to solve the problems of public service cuts. Promote this work with writing and photos online and through social networks. These meetings are retributive, and therefore do not liaise with the city as represented by the EM. Collaboration is predicated on the restoration of a democratically elected government in Flint.

...withhold paying any taxes to the State of Michigan until the removal of Flint's EM, effective immediately.

THE TALE OF THE WATER OF LIFE

Collected by the Brothers Grimm
Reinterpreted by Connor Coyne

Originally published in Moomers Journal of Moomers Studies
9 (April 2015)

Prior to publication, this story was displayed as part of a carnival installation
for the Flint Order of Orpheus (FLOOR)
February 2015

Once upon a time there lived a king named Oceanus who ruled over the land of Arrowhead. One day, he grew very sick with a mysterious illness. His three sons – Prince Benthos, Prince Pelagos, and Prince Riparian – grief-stricken at their father's illness, went out of the castle into a beautiful garden, and wept.

An old man happened to be passing by, and he asked the young men, "why are you crying?" and they said, "it is because our father is ill. He has grown very sick and nobody knows how to make him well again. He is dying, and that is why we are sad!"

"There is a cure for every disease," said the old man. "You must give him the Water of Life, which resides at Castle Perculsa across the ocean."

Prince Benthos – the eldest – went to the king and told him about the Water of Life, but the king shook his shaggy head and said, "no, no, you must not go. That path is too dangerous." But Benthos believed that if he could find the cure, his father would leave him the keys to the kingdom when he died, and then Benthos would rule over all of Arrowhead. He crept out, secretly, and took the road that led toward Castle Perculsa.

A day along his journey, he passed a sad-faced man with one foot who said, "where are you going in such a hurry?"

"None of your damn business!" snapped Benthos, and he shoved the man to the ground.

Next, Prince Benthos came to a thicket of raspberry bushes and, charging in, he became entangled in the briars so that he couldn't go forward and he couldn't go backward.

Weeks passed.

Now, Prince Pelagos went to his father and asked permission to seek the Water of Life, but the king told him it was too dangerous. But Pelagos believed that if he found the cure and his brother had died, Oceanus would leave him the keys to the kingdom, and then Pelagos would rule over all of Arrowhead. The guards blocked the exit, but Pelagos made a rope out of his clothing, climbed out a window, and set off in search of the Water of Life.

A day along his journey, he passed the one-footed man who said, "what's the matter?"

"Shut up, you!" shouted Pelagos, and kicked the man's walking stick out from under him, so that the man fell on his face.

Next, Prince Pelagos came to a fetid swamp and, charging in, he became mired in the muck so that he couldn't go forward and he couldn't go backward.

Weeks passed.

Finally, Prince Riparian went to his father and asked permission to seek the Water of Life, but Oceanus warned him it was too dangerous.

"But now I have lost my brothers," said Riparian, "and the Water of Life is our only hope. Must I lose you too?"

This touched King Oceanus and, reluctantly, he let his last son depart.

A day along his journey, Prince Riparian passed the one-footed man who asked, "why do you look so worried?"

"I am worried because my father is dying," answered the young prince. "The only way I can save him is with the Water of Life."

"You are a good son, who worries about his father's health, so I will tell you what you need to know. When you come to the raspberry bushes, do not go through them but turn to the left. When you come to the mud, do not go through it but turn to the right. Then when you come to the gates of Castle Perculsa, strike it three times with this iron rod. The gate will open. You will see a hungry dog, but throw it this sack of tidbits. Then enter the castle courtyard, where you will find the Water of Life flowing from a fountain. Fill this clay pot, and leave before the clock strikes twelve. At midnight, the gates will swing shut, and nobody can escape from the castle."

Prince Riparian thanked the man, taking with him the iron rod, the sack of tidbits, and the clay pot.

As he went on, he reached the raspberry bushes, but took the path to the left. He reached the mud and took the path to the right. Then, Riparian came to Castle Perculsa. He struck the iron gate three times with the iron rod, and the gate swung open. There stood a hungry dog, angry and howling, but Riparian threw the dog the sack of tidbits, and it ate them up and went away with its tail wagging. Riparian entered the castle and in the first courtyard he found a beautiful princess with a sassy look on her face. "My name's Maxine and this is my vacation cottage," she said, "how did you make it past the gate and the dog? You look like you're of marriageable age. Did you bring me a dowry? Anyway, feel free to make yourself at home. There is a room with deadly weapons, there is a room with fresh bread, and there is a room with a luxurious bed, there is a room with precious jewels, and there is a fountain filled with the Water of Life."

Prince Riparian went in, exploring the castle. It was cold but elegant and perfect. Frost-covered tapestries hung from the walls. Ice sculptures of courtiers bowed and curtsied from atop their blue pedestals. Then the prince came to the room with the fresh bread, and he took a loaf from the table. He came to the room filled with deadly weapons and he took the sharpest sword. He came to the room with precious jewels and took the brightest ring. Finally, he came to the room with the luxurious bed, and he was very tired, and lay down to rest.

It was a good sleep and he dreamed happy dreams. He dreamed of his happy father, healed of his illness, and his older bothers, proud and beaming. Riparian dreamed of the elegant Princess Maxine, asking for his hand in marriage and accepting his dowry. He dreamt of the Water of Life, cool, clean, healthy and affordable, well-suited to the hydration of dried-out cells and the curing of unfortunate illnesses. He dreamt of swimming in clear pools and cupping the crystals that lay at the bottom. It was a good dream.

Prince Riparian woke up at quarter to midnight. He leapt from the bed and ran through the castle until he found the room with the fountain filled with the Water of Life. The prince hurriedly filled the clay pot, then ran back through the castle until he reached the gate. Riparian slipped through the gate just as the clock struck twelve and as that heavy steel portal swung shut, it pinched Riparian's ankle and cut his right foot clean off. He wrapped the stump in willow leaves to staunch his loss of blood. He fashioned a walking stick out of a elder branch and turned his back on Castle Perculsa. He didn't mind leaving the castle behind, but he was having a hard time forgetting Princess Maxine, her skill at Risk and Diplomacy and Go Fish, her cunning eyes, her sharp wit. But his mind turned toward his ailing father, and he went along as quickly as he was able.

On his way back home, Prince Riparian passed the one-footed man again, who said, "you lost your foot, just as I lost mine! But you have gotten a great loaf of bread. You can tear it and tear it, but it will never run out. And you have gotten a great sword. With that single sword you could defeat an entire army. I also see that you have gotten a gorgeous ring. That ring can carve out stabilizing currency to resolve the direst fiscal crisis."

"But I have not found my brothers, and I am afraid that they are dead!"

Now the one-footed man felt guilty, for he knew what had happened to Prince Benthos and Prince Pelagos. The man told Riparian about their prisons in the wilderness, and so he freed them from the brambles and the mud and, reunited, the three princes continued on the road home.

First, they passed through the Black Land, which was in the midst of a terrible famine, but Prince Riparian lent the queen his loaf of bread, and she used it to feed the entire kingdom. The brothers continued on their way.

Second, they passed through the Red Land which was midst of a terrible war, but Prince Riparian lent the queen his sword, and she used it to slaughter her enemies in the land. The brothers continued on their way.

Third, they passed through the Silver Land, which was in the grip of hyperinflation, but Prince Riparian lent the queen his ring, and she used it to create stabilizing currency and restore the economy to order. The brothers continued on their way.

Then they got on a ship and sailed down the river to the Kingdom of Arrowhead.

The waters swirled beneath the prow of the boat, and Prince Benthos said to Prince Pelagos, "I want to rule the kingdom, but our brother has that sword, and our father will think he is the most powerful ruler, and let him rule the kingdom instead."

And Prince Pelagos said to Prince Benthos, "*I* want to rule the kingdom, but our brother has that loaf of bread, and our father will think he is the wisest ruler, and let him rule the kingdom instead."

And each brother said to the other, "We want to rule Arrowhead, but our brother has that ring, and our father will think that he is the most fiscally prudent, and one who takes audacious economic initiative under dire circumstances, squeezing money from a rock, and will thus let him rule the kingdom instead."

So the two princes decided that they must create a scandal for Prince Riparian.

While Riparian lay sleeping under the stars, his brothers took the clay pot filled with the Water of Life, and poured it into two glass phials. Then they filled the clay pot with overchlorinated river water.

Eventually, the three princes made it back home and Riparian took the clay pot directly to King Oceanus. The king took a drink, but immediately spit it out again. "This is disgusting!" he announced. "This water is rusted-out and discolored. It was formerly filled with E. Coli bacteria and presently with excessive Trihalomethanes. Why did you go on such a long journey and at such expense just to bring me some disgusting water?"

Then the older two brothers burst into the room and accused Prince Riparian of trying to poison the king. "You wanted to kill him so you could rule the kingdom yourself!" they said. "So you tried to poison him before we could give him the real Water of Life."

Then the two older sons gave the king their phials of water, and the king drank it and felt better at once.

Now King Oceanus thought that Riparian had tried to poison him, and he was quite wroth, so he called the Royal Huntsman and told the man to take the prince into the forest and stab him in the heart. The Huntsman rolled his eyes at the king and said, "sure."

But when the Huntsman and the youngest son arrived in the forest, the Huntsman set his knife on a fallen log, and sat down, and started crying. Riparian said, "you look miserable! What's wrong?"

"I've been ordered to stab you in the heart, my prince!"

"Ahhhhhh!"

"Ahhhhhh!"

"Who ordered you to do this?"

"Your father, the king!"

"Ahhhhhh!"

"Ahhhhhh!"

"Zounds! But why would my kind father want to do this to me? I'll bet that my evil brothers are behind this plot. I should have left them in the mud and the raspberry bushes! You won't stab me, will you?"

"Have you ever heard of a Huntsman in a fairy tale executing an innocent in cold blood."

"Indeed, I have not."

"We never do. We are consistently good folk. Here, take my common clothes and flee into the Thetford Wilderness. You will not be recognized as the prince. I will offer the king the heart of a toad as proof of your assassination. You will be safe and free."

And the prince took Huntsman's clothes and limped off into the wilderness.

Meanwhile, back in Arrowhead, King Oceanus was surprised by the arrival of a caravan full of glistening onyx, led by the Black Queen.

"Why have you sent this?" the king asked.

"Your son Prince Riparian saved my kingdom from famine. I send these gifts out of gratitude."

A few days later, the king was surprised by the arrival of a caravan full of brilliant rubies, led by the Red Queen.

"Why have you sent this?" the king asked.

"Your son Prince Riparian saved my kingdom from war. I send these gifts out of gratitude."

Three days later, the king was somewhat less surprised by the arrival of a caravan full of glittering diamonds, led by the Silver Queen.

"Why have you sent this?" the king asked.

"Your son Prince Riparian saved my kingdom from hyperinflation. I send these gifts out of gratitude."

The king summoned his Huntsman.

"I fear that I have made a terrible mistake," Oceanus said. "I think that I might have been tricked by the worthless Benthos and Pelagos into betraying my youngest son. I fear that I have misjudged him. And here I had you murder him. If only I could undo that terrible deed."

"Haven't you ever read a fairy tale?" asked the Huntsman. "We Huntsman don't kill people. We're a terrible choice for a hit job. I gave your son my commoners' clothes and sent him off to live off the scraps of the land in the formidable Thetford Wilderness."

While these intrigues unfolded in the court of the Kingdom of Arrowhead, other matters developed in Castle Perculsa. Princess Maxine had thought the matter through from several angles, cunning and sincere, and she decided that Prince Riparian was of a marriageable age, that he presumably had accumulated an impressive dowry for her through the judicious use of the sword, bread, and rings, and also that she loved him, carnally and romantically. She opened the front gate and ordered her retainers to build a golden road from the castle to the river, knowing that, if the good prince was worthy, he would walk straight up the road, looking neither to the left nor the right.

As it turns out, Prince Benthos and Prince Pelagos had also set out in search of Castle Perculsa. They had envied their brother his ring and bread and sword and figured that there must be more treasures that they could take and exploit.

When the Prince Benthos came to Maxine's golden road, he thought that it would be a crime to tarnish the glimmery smooth surface with his thorny boots, so he walked to the right of the road until he came to the castle. The retainers shut the door in his face.

When the Prince Pelagos came to Maxine's golden road, he thought that it would be a sin to streak the glinty bright surface with his muddy boots, so he walked to the left of the road until he came to the castle. The retainers slammed the door on him.

Now Prince Riparian had been dreaming about Princess Maxine throughout his wretched exile in the vile Thetford wilderness. She walked in his dreams every night and smiled at him, and gave him prudent advice, and eventually he decided that he must find her and declare his undying affection for her. So Riparian set off again for Castle Perculsa, leaning on his walking stick all the while. So enamored was Riparian of the princess, that he noticed nothing about him; not the raspberry brambles, nor the muddy bog, nor the road paved with golden bricks. Riparian marched straight up the road and the guards let him into the castle.

"You have come!" said his princess.

"I have come!" said her prince.

And they were married at once and celebrated the carnival and the Mardi Gras with beads and doubloons and masks and costumes and cakes and wine and excess. Yes! Together they enjoyed many successes in life, having many children, seeing many exotic lands, making many wise and fruitful investments, and drinking pure, clean water each day. Arrowhead flourished. All things considered, Queen Maxine and King Riparian lived happily, happily ever after.

Not so for Prince Benthos and Prince Pelagos. They were apprehended not far from Castle Perculsa, taken far up into the mountains, and hurled from a cliff at devastating heights. They shrieked as they fell, their arms pinwheeling wildly, their eyes as wide as a blue Fiesta saucer that drinks in the dew on the cusp of its doom, until their chests were cloven in twain upon twin jagged obsidian promontories emerging from the ledges below. The spikes managed to puncture their lungs while missing their hearts and garrote their necks without slashing their throats. Then, the scarred and wailing princes fell again, rolled down the mountainside, down the foothills, and down the little hills, their bodies beaten and broken by rocks and stones until they came to rest at the edge of a bog. They struggled to stand, to lift themselves to their feet, but their ragged and dislocated arms wouldn't support their own weight. The sun rose and scorched their naked backs until they broke out in blisters, and insects swarmed down and feasted upon the festering boils. Streams of blood, copper red in that hellish blazing sun called down the vultures who circled, waiting for death's arrival, while hawks and eagles dove down on the brothers and took off with clumps of their hair and scalp, and plucked their eyeballs from their skulls, and nibbled at their chapped lips, and gorged themselves on royal fingers and toes. Just a few feet away, the swamp water, fetid as it was, called to the two princes, offering some relief to their thirst, their parched throats. This wasn't the Water of Life, nay, it was infused with E. Coli and Trihalomthanes and rust and even other nasty things, but at least it was wet. But that window of opportunity had passed, for now Benthos and Pelagos were altogether too weak to even drag themselves such a miniscule distance. After hours, days, weeks, months, and years of lying in great torment, a storm came down upon the marsh, dark clouds and torrential rains that caused the banks of the bog to swell. Finally, the princes thought, they might get a drink at last and enjoy some small measure of relief before they expired from their wounds.

But before they could soothe their aching throats, lightning struck them and reduced them to ash.

Originally published in Moria Poetry Zine, 12, no. 3
(Winter 2010)

The mutt yawned so expansively that one could look far down its throat into brown, cavernous depths. Frank sat in his chair by the Space Heater and pet the dog. Across the room, Beatrice applied the cherry flavored lip balm May had given her. Beatrice's waxy finger smelled like candy, and she licked it lightly. She leaned back, pulled a blanket around her knees, and looked out the window. Still a little snow on the ground. One block away, she saw the paperboy, his arms plunged into his pockets. He had delivered his papers. He was headed home. He stared through his frosty breath down the road he walked.

It was this boy for whom Beatrice's affections had so recently stirred. Stirring as in to take a wooden sp corn oil in the small ti ugar soaked in ound the rim of

"This boy," boy. I don' that. That's what? He's a ing out. That's

The anger concern we her fingers anger and the them to warm

"If I find an

The sun be sunlight sh e o'clock. The

"I'll never g

"If I ever fir

Beatrice lo stamping h furnace wo that boy was and hoped the

I never had May would hoped that the gravel. etroleum jelly," r, but I secretly wn and kick up

Orsino's problem is entirely his reluctance to celebrate Valentines Day. His personal feelings notwith- standing it *is* just a holiday, and who does he expect to hurt by celebrating a holiday he holds in no regard? And any- way... if he wants to win the girl, then he'll have to convince her father. Orsino doesn't realize what a hard sell the man is. This is not a man to set a strict curfew so much as set his dogs upon you. To gnaw at you.

"How do you think you know?" Frank asked.

"Oh. I know."

The next morning, the furnace started working.

DASH AGAINST DARKNESS

Originally published in Santa Clara Review, 96, no. 2
(Spring/Summer 2009)

When I negotiate for compass points, my argument's a biased vanity. The western hills of Kettering disappoint, and I was born with sunlight in the east. If to the south blues shiver all night long, the Eastside parking lots pick up the sound. If to the north the churches shake with song, the Eastside factories listen and resound. And if tall buildings still light up downtown, the lights out east are never dark or dim. We meditate beneath the lunar round and, in the morning, lift the sun again. But if you think my compass is askew: listen. The old die. And the born are new.

* * * * *

"I've been waiting. I've waited. For so long. Can we send? With a dove?"

"A pigeon."

"A dove?"

"A pigeon."

"Okay then. With a pigeon."

"..."

"Is it going to be alright?"

"..."

* * * * *

Gerald sat up in bed.

His Margery had left him. Her Gerald was left behind.

The truth of this fact was clear as he examined his arm in the mirror. No name on the arm. No name in the reflection. Just himself. Where had she gone?

Now in the kitchen. Boiling the water for the ramen. Old flowers, dead for a long time, sitting in a vase on the windowsill above the sink. He tossed them in the garbage. It was still morning, barely. But he felt tired. Why did he feel tired? He rubbed his eyes. Somehow, he knew it was going to be a long day. Gerald's clothes, scattered on the living room floor. Margery's clothes, neatly folded in boxes in the attic.

Back in the bathroom. Rubbing his eyes. Looking at them in the mirror. Red somehow. From his rubbing. Or maybe his allergies. It was late September, the beginning of autumn, but after a couple frosts and a rainy smell (clouds straight out to nowhere) the leaves were already turning. Already falling. Dazzling, yes, rivers of crimson and gold that drowned themselves in the asphalt curb rivers. But why couldn't it be spring, with finned maple seeds helicoptering down? Why not summer, at the Farmers Market with a coriander smoke puffing up along the aisle? Why not? Why wasn't his Margery here? Why had she left him? Why had she gone?

Only one thing to do.

Gerald turned on the shower, and when the steam had grown so dense that it coated the mirror and made him into a wraithly shape, he undressed and stepped in. The water banged against his head. He ran his arms slick against the skin. Wiped the water back, but little trickles still wound down his forehead and found his eyes. He turned into the stream, opened mouth. He gargled the falling water, and it water bubbled out as if from an overflowing drainage pipe. No one to ridicule him for this. No one to tease him or taunt him as hopelessly unfastidious. The house was empty except for Gerald and the noise he made.

Only one thing to do.

He opened the window to let in a breath of the cold outside air. He looked out into the backyard. Grass gleaming in the gray rain, beneath the gray sky. Pink and pastel orange leaves clinging, but just barely, to the pear tree. The red tips and numbs of his beets poking at an angle from the dirt. The chain link fence. Behind that, poplar trees, yellow, with fast bark, wrinkled bark. Behind, the neighbor's yard. Someone played R&B very loudly. Why don't they turn it up louder? he thought. He thought he saw someone dancing on the other side of a yellow window, but it was all hazy in the rain. Why don't they come outside and dance? Gerald shut the window, shut off the shower, and stopped out onto the pink bathmat. It dried his feet. He toweled his head dry and wiped the mirror clean.   He shaved and looked at his arm. He toweled himself dry. Every last bit of rangy chest hair. He slapped on some stinging aftershave, wiped Old Spice across his armpits, toweled his heavy crotch some more. Pulled the towel between his buttocks then, horizontal, across his back. It's so hard to get dry, he thought. He dressed. From the kitchen, something hissed and sputtered, then spat like static. It was the pot of ramen boiling over. A pigeon landed on the gutter outside. "You have to seek her out."

Only one thing to do.

He'd have to go outside.

He was all alone in the shower steam, in the rainy day. He had to go out and find her.

* * * * *

Gerald stepped out onto his porch.

He was afraid.

The roof hung over the porch and framed the front yard, and the gray rain made a neat curtain, grim and translucent, for a riot of fallen leaves. They sparkled like diamonds but drifted like mote, doomed. The empty black streets and lustrous fire hydrants. Some kids stamped through a puddle up the way and sang a song they'd memorized together, but Gerald was terrified.

It was a feeling. Would he ever see his house again? The lock asked him this. The key rotated against its catch, a slight torque, small but metallic and firm enough to slide the deadbolt home. No, probably not, said the key. Bright brass hidden beneath the cracking, warping wood. The porch asked him as it creaked beneath his feet. He turned right onto the sidewalk and started walking away. He looked back two houses down. His own house, it seemed to sag and say "goodbye."

Gerald didn't want to go alone; he was horrified to think he might go alone. What if I don't find her? What if she's hidden? What if she doesn't want me to find her? Or what if I get lost on the way?

It was almost enough to make him turn back.

Amity, Gerald thought. Amity will come with me. So he turned toward Amity's house. He walked past the church parking plot, packed with rusting cars. They had gathered for an old priest's funeral. He reached a corner where a car pulled up to the Drive-Thru liquor store, blasting Gloria Gaynor. He continued, and as he walked, he thought of Amity.

Gerald had known Amity ever since they were children growing up on the Eastside. Sometimes Gerald had ridden his trike over to Amity's and the two had made mud pies in the back yard ruts where the puddles were deep and chocolate. Not much later, Amity's mother would escort her to Gerald's house where his older brother watched them both for the evening while the parents went bowling or dancing. Of course, Gerald and Amity hadn't seen each other as much later on, when Amity went to college and Gerald turned to the factory, but he'd visited her often, and on one trip, she'd introduced him to Margery.

Amity had been a bridesmaid at their wedding, and so many years later, the three of them had often gotten together to play cards or see a movie.

Gerald walked under the overpass and Amity's house swung into view, a two-story aluminum-sided tower pressed between daisy choked vacant lots. Something was off, however; the lights were dark. Strange, Gerald thought. Amity was usually home on a Tuesday. He walked up onto the porch and rang the doorbell. He waited. The house creaked above him, around him. It groaned sternly, like a security guard's bored repetitions that "the building is closed; you'll have to come back tomorrow." Gerald waited, studied the dark shadows in the windows and tried again. Still, groans then silence. Gerald walked around to the side of the house and knocked on the side door. No answer. He stepped back into the driveway, turned toward the house, cupped his hands at his mouth and called: "Amity!" Then he walked back to the sidewalk, faced the house, cupped hands at mouth and called:

"Amity! Come out! I need you to go with me to look for Margery! I woke up this morning and she was gone!"

The house groaned and creaked some more and the wind huffed by. Gerald's best friend was evidently away, Tuesday notwithstanding. Gerald started walking back toward the overpass. He thought, though, that maybe he ought to try one more time. When he turned around he saw a pale hand release a milk-stained curtain. The second-story front. The curtain fell back into place, and the room behind it was hidden. Gerald lifted his arm toward the window, showing Amity the blank space where his tattoo had been. He turned and left again.

* * * * *

It hurt and stung Gerald that Amity would not come out to help him. He did not know why she was frightened of him and his questions nor, if afraid, why her love for Margery and himself did not drive her out onto the front porch and force her to ask what was wrong.

She'd been a bridesmaid, after all.

The wind chilled Gerald as he walked along Lewis, parallel to the expressway, past ramshackle businesses, plywood fronts, and Indiana limestone with kaleidoscope graffiti. Gerald made himself smile. If a bridesmaid lacked devotion, then perhaps a Maid of Honor and a Best Man would understand. Andrew and Adelpha, Gerald's brother and sister lived just south in the East Village. He'd always helped them clean their rooms when they were out with their friends. At night, when the meal was finished, when Andrew washed the dishes and Adelpha rinsed, Gerald dried and put away. The three had worked in the shop together for some years, and they had dozens if not hundreds of barbecues and fishing trips under their belts. They'd gone camping with Gerald and Margery, and together, the four had faced the bright and icy spray of Tahquamenon Falls. Andrew and Adelpha would come with him, wherever he ended up going.

Eventually, Gerald crossed into a neighborhood with larger yards and neater houses. He found his siblings' house and knocked on the front door. Andrew came to the door.

"Gerald," he said.

"Andrew," Gerald said. "She's gone." And Gerald showed his arm.

"So she is," Andrew said, and Adelpha came to stand at his side.

"Who is gone?" Adelpha asked.

Gerald showed his arm.

"Oh," said Adelpha.

"I'm going for her," Gerald said. "I'm going."

They waited, there, on the porch. The rain fell. Wind chimes shivered together, ringing soft. The porch swing moved back and forth.

"Is she coming back?" Andrew asked.

"I guess that depends on where I find her."

"No, Gerald," said Adelpha with a soft, comforting, honeyed voice. "No."

"Are you going to come back?" Andrew asked.

"Depends on when I find her," Gerald said.

But Adelpha shook her head.

"I need you to come with me," Gerald said.

More waiting.

"We can't go," said Andrew. Throat tight. "I can't go, I mean."

"Why can't you come with me?"

"Because..."

"Because?"

"Because..."

"Yes?"

"There is a church banquet tomorrow night. There's a fund raiser for the Moose Lodge. A meeting of Downtown Development. St. Michael's and the metal stamping union group. Someone has to show up with the coffee."

More waiting.

"Adelpha?" Gerald asked.

"Oh, Gerald," she said. "My knees. You know they're so weak. I have a hard enough time getting up and down those stairs. I couldn't make it past the first block, especially in this rain."

"But I can drive you!" said Gerald, ragged voiced. They looked at him. "I can buy you coffee to take tomorrow."

More waiting.

"You were my Best Man. Her Maid of Honor."

And waiting...

"My brother and sister!"

But Adelpha let go of the door's molding. She retreated into the small, white house, watching. And then Andrew receded, eyes cool and glassy. He gave a slight nod as he shut the door. Behind him, in the dark rooms of the house, the crowds cheered on The Price is Right. A cuckoo called out the time. The door shut.

* * * * *

Fine then. Fine then, Gerald thought. People grew old and dissolved. Gerald knew that; he had watched it for over sixty years. He hadn't expected their souls or hearts to dissolve, no, but he held himself forth as proof of an exception. If his friends and family wouldn't accompany him, then he'd supply himself with all the necessary supplies. He'd head into the wilderness alone. He wouldn't stop looking for Margery. He wouldn't. He wouldn't. He wouldn't stop looking until she was there and their pinky fingers entwined.

Gerald continued on. He took the mossy path between the elms on the Greenway then walked along the close-cut grass of the Eastside where the stumps stuck up at even intervals. He crossed the expressway and followed the road as it wound down on a dusty margin past the milk bottling plant, the Holiday Inn, the post-office and, ultimately, toward the river. It would be riding high in this rain, but where was the rain going?

It seemed less...

He entered the Farmers' Market. The awning folded over him and he found himself inside a long green pavilion with steamed windows converging in the distance. The space was packed thick with people: moms and dads, children in strollers, and old women squeezing the fruit to test whether it was firm enough.

Gerald stood and breathed in and out. He went shopping:

The rutabagas, turnips, sprouting beets,
cloudy full bags of chickens feet and beef,
tins of fishing grubs and strands of wheat,
tomatoes swollen, wet potatoes, milk,
cucumbers, bone white cloves of garlic, trout,
bananas, rice, parsnips and oranges, pears,

whole and drawn and pan-dressed, vinegar, trout,
cereal, corn, muffins, brownies, wheat,
pumpkin pie, cake, steaming pink cuts of beef,
cherry pie from Traverse city, pears,
rhubarb pie, thick shelled brown eggs, celery, beets,
apple crisp, a bundt cake, cookies and milk,

spaghetti, knotty mushrooms, knotty pears,
wet cauliflower and carrots, salted beets,
green peas, bell peppers, green peppers, smoked trout,
rump roast, rib roast, flank steak, skirt steak, ground beef,
black beans, wet cheddar, crackers and whole milk,
pineapples, kiwi, coconut, dry wheat,

cauliflower, cabbage, eggplant, goat's milk,
gourds and melons, veal, venison, trout,
marshmallows and lemons, limes and red beets,
French bread, Italian bread, black bread and wheat,
pumpkin, rhubarb, cherry, grapes, red pears,
spinach, squash, brown sugar, perch and beef,

dried oats and pumpernickel rye and wheat,
drowsy bran and wormholed fleshy pears,
cranberries, peaches, onions, luscious milk,
half milk, skim milk, Colby, vinegar beets,
Flanken-style ribs and bluegill, raw beef,
branching broccoli stalks, heaving, gasping trout,

turkey, walnuts, chicken, chestnuts, ham, beef,
leeks, mace, snap peas, chick peas, cow's milk,
red peppers, gooseberries, dates, flour, fat pears,
pomegranate meringue, sardines and trout,
beer from barley, wine and bourbon and wheat,
waxed beans, jellybeans and ambrosial beets.

A sandwich of beef and fillet of trout
with a cup of milk. A slice of bread, wheat.
A plateful of beets. A bowlful of pears.

Gerald was prepared.

Arms dripping sacks full of food and produce, he set off toward the river. The rain had stopped now, and the quilt of the clouds had been pulled back from overhead... now the vague circle of the afternoon cast its bright haze through the translucent sheets overhead. Gerald reached the river. The world was not quite as cold and steely looking as before. But where do I go now? he wondered. A pigeon landed. "You can't take that with you."

Gerald stood and looked out at the muddy current rolling and roiling by. It was wet, and so he started to cry. He moved down. Knelt like an altar boy. Let the bags drop from his hands. Beets and pears rolled out onto the grass. "You can't take that with you."

"Then what?"

"You can't take that with you."

"Then what can I take with me?"

"Dash against darkness."

"Where have I heard that before?"

"Dash against darkness."

"Fine."

Gerald stood again. He knew his eyes were red from crying. Some bicyclists rode past. He thought that they must be staring at them. He stared back. They rode past. They hadn't noticed him at all. Overhead, poplars. They rose and roared. The sky cleared further. Gerald didn't want to head out alone. But Margery had already left. He had to find her and nobody would come with him. He couldn't even take his beef and trout, pears and beets.

Fine, he thought. If it has to be it has to be. Sugar beets. Goodbye beets.

And he continued along the river bank.

Fine then! he thought. I will find you Margery! I will look and look and look until I find you, and then, my wife, we will hook our pinky fingers together and kiss.

* * * * *

* * * * *

But this morning. This morning Gerald had gotten up and noticed a peculiar lack of itching on his right arm. Strange, he'd thought. That arm's itched every morning since... many years. Over forty years. He looked at his arm. Just the night before it had displayed a tattoo: a lovely girl, seventeen years old, dark hair and pearls. She wore a pearl dress, and cradled in her arms a beet and a pear. In a filigree above her crown, her name:

Margery

That was when he knew that she was somewhere, she was, and he just had to go and find her.

More, he knew without a doubt, for this was an unambiguous sign, that the time had arrived to seek her out.

But he didn't want to go alone. It's frightening, seeking out one who has died, and he wasn't sure what he'd come upon going on his own.

"So don't."

Gerald looked up and there he was, leaning against the nearest cottonwood. He was twenty, perhaps. Thirty. Forty. He'd never been a handsome man. He had sharp, serious, mournful gray eyes... those eyes could turn eyes, sure. But his nose was too hawklike, his ears too big and shellish.

His hair, a mess of stiff sticks, it was sweat damp until he was fifty, and then it all fell out.

"You're me," Gerald said. "If you go with me, I'm still going alone. Besides, I take myself with me wherever I go."

"I guess that means you're never alone," Gerald said.

Gerald shrugged.

They continued along the river.

"What does this mean?" Gerald asked. "Is this death or something? Is this dying or something? Am I officially walking toward the white light?"

"Probably shouldn't think of it like that. But it isn't as gloomy as it was this morning. Look, the sun's coming out."

It had, through a pocket in the clouds. There were more pockets, gradually. More frequently. Gerald and Gerald followed the river and it turned like a snake, flat and flexing back toward the milk bottling plant. They stopped under the shade of an apple tree. A cricket chirped nearby.

"This is where you must leave the others behind," said Gerald.

"What others?" asked Gerald. "Nobody came with me."

And then he realized he'd been mistaken.

Other Geralds surrounded them.

Here was Gerald the Shop-Worker, who welded and rigged and had trouble hearing his coworkers through the safety-goggles that fit awkwardly over his head, folding the flaps of his heavy ears back against his head. This Gerald had heavy rough hands that could tame sparks.

And here was Gerald the Church Member, who always thought that slacks and a sweater was good enough, even when Margery wore her spring dress, and the two walked up the stairs like a rosebush with a hawthorn. But he was a good listener, that Gerald, and thoughtful.

And Uncle Gerald, a good listener like Church Gerald, but a bit more patient and less judgmental. Not quite as serious and grim about the world.

Here were the ears of Gerald, half asleep where he stood, half-ignoring the conversation around him.

Here were the eyes of Gerald, deep and soft and sharp and gray, constantly studying the changes in the world.

And Young Gerald. Gerald's discretion, calmly listening on the phone to some catastrophe described from the other end. Strong Gerald, carrying his father back up the basement stairs, and cupping his head so that blood didn't flow. The Prime Gerald, the handsomest one, sitting down by the river, this same river, admiring the fireflies on a steamy night in June. And a favorite, Gerald the Gardener, hands full and rich and grainy with the black earth.

"Will I find her?" Gerald asked.

"You're procrastinating!" they answered. "You're procrastinating!"

"But will I find her?" Gerald asked.

"Don't put it off," they answered.

"I just want to find her."

And waiting.

Clouds dissipated.

"Why can't you all come with me?"

"We can't. If you want to find Margery, you have to leave all this behind: the shop and the church and the kids and the garden. Your eyes your lips your ears your tongue. All go, all go. Leave gone go. You might as well go."

"Will I find her?"

"Your good looks and your strength and discretion. Your senses and your beauty and your moments and memories. You have to leave this all behind."

"Then how will I find Margery?"

"I'll help you find Margery."

"Why do you get to come with me?"

"I'm you. How are you going to leave you behind?"

"It would seem I am leaving myself behind."

"No. None of that's you. That is all you, but it's all that is acquired and lost."

"What is acquired and lost?"

"Not what swells and grows together. Not what merges."

The sun exploded from behind the clouds and entered a sea-vast ocean of sky.

* * * * *

Gerald wandered the Eastside for many minutes, hours, days, weeks, months, years. He walked from the brink of the curb of the projects on Atherton clear north to the slippery algae skim of the reservoir. Beef and trout. He took himself with him, and while things fluctuated and changed, while identity was never solid but sleek, shimmering, effervescent, floating, dissolving, bubbling, breaking, and bursting, he was never alone. He kept himself company. The conversation left something to be desired; Gerald was never a good conversationalist, and he kept his comments to a "yes" and a "no," a grunt about the weather, or most often, about whether he would find Margery. What would she be wearing? And would he look rough and uncouth as usual? Would she frown at him? She always hated when he was sloppy.

A few times, he asked others, shop owners, bicyclists, kids hanging on the corner, for directions. But gradually, day by day, Gerald realized he didn't need directions, and whether he lost interest in these people or whether they stopped noticing him was something almost unconsidered.

In Kearsley Park, the sun drove west behind the expressway and factories. The stars came out over the huge vast pavilion with sets for *The Merchant of Venice* or *Timon of Athens*. Ice Cream trucks piped along a few blocks away and the hornets crawled along dropped cups of ice cream and honey. Milk.

Before dawn at Angelo's Coney Island, the steamy dishwater coffee cups stuck to the greasy tables and the clock reflected off the window, floating phantomlike against the naked storefronts across the street, and backwards upside-down numbers hovered in puddles on the cratered parking lot. Wheat.

September had become August somehow.

One bright morning day, Gerald was walking along the bank of the river and a pigeon alighted.

I don't have any bread for you," he said. It was the first thing he'd said in weeks. The pigeon pecked about, curious.

Gerald listened for Gerald's reply. But Gerald didn't reply. And then he realized he was gone. Nowhere. Something had ceased to be, he thought. Or maybe, he wondered, though he didn't want to hope, since hope always seemed to teach disappointment, nevertheless, something had merged, just as Gerald had once said. The sun set somewhere, and August was becoming something else. Gerald thought he saw beets poking up from the ground and pears dripping from above. Is this? he wondered, less than a voice. To his surprise, his arm tingled with a needle's pressure and then a voice answered:

"There you are at last," she said. "Are you ready?"

Excerpt from
TODAY'S YOUTH ISN'T LAZY,
THEY'RE JUST DEPRESSED

*A novel published on connorcoyne.com each day
during May 2013, between 12 and 3 AM, EDT.
The novel has been offline since May 2013, although it is
briefly published for twenty-four hours each April.*

CHAPTER 6 IS THE TEXTUAL CHAPTER...

The sky was gray because the sun was getting ready to come up.

Krista pressed her wet nose againsty the icy cold window, looking for the garbage truck. She couldn't see it, but she could hear it, rumbling somewhere out of sight, its pistons hissing as they crushed garbage into wrinkled white cubes. That was how she imagined it.

Somewhere in the house, Charles and Candace were disputing. Krista couldn't see them, but she could hear them, her mom's voice sharp, her grandpa's voice gravelly, rolling out of the gloomy gray.

"Listen," Candace was saying, "I know you want to help out. I do. But there are things you don't understand and I can't get antithing done – away – each day, if I'm worrying about what you'll do."

"Peanut lardy and jelly sandwich," Charles answered. "Macaroni and cheese. Tuna fish sandwiches. Caramel chunk cookies –"

"You've never made cookies before in your life!"

"Durian. Bananas. Kiwi. Kumquat. Bananas –"

"You just said bananas!"

"Pork stroganoff."

Krista watched a vapor grow over the glass as she exhaled. Cozy with the cold, she knew that the trash out there was stinky trash. The way pink giblet liquid slid out onto the white trash containers. The way the boibled bubbles puddled on the wet railings. But the garbage truck would come and take it all away. Mama was going away, too. Mama said she was going up the road to apply therely McDonalds. Krista knew a lot of words, but she didn't quite know that word "apply." She wouldn't have recognized the letters. It was all about the sounds: "Up ply." She thought that it might have something to do withthattthereairplane, this important thing that Mama was going to exist done that day. "Just a little," she had said over McDonalds the night before. "Improved than nothing," she had said. "Krista, teethgrind your McNuggets."

"Your mother used to heat good food here," Charles had said. "Wonderful food. Nothing like this. Not fast food."

"We consumified out sometimes," Candace had answered, iterated adjact its grizzley adjudication.

"No we didn't," Charles answered. "Not McDonalds. Not fast food."

"Look," she said. "You got mustard all over your chin. Oh, Baal, you got it all over your shirt."

And just like a mama with a toddler, Candace had wadded up her napkin and tongued it, and swiped stone to shine up the trouble on Charles' stubbly chin and white undershirt.

Krista had giggled.

Candace had hissed.

Charles had looked on with peekers so, so sad.

But that was yesterday.

Or the day before.

Krista didn't know.

This prebright, Charles was on the maraud.

"It's a nowhere job!"

"Look," Candace said, "there's no reason you can't help too. You remember that jobby I was telling you about. You can make money online. Get online, just like I told you to –"

"I don't like to."

"– chase all of their memoranda very discretionarily–"

"What are you going to do?"

"– make absolute to examine the grammar before you shoot out antidescriptors –"

"What are you going to do?"

"– and you can make us a mite of money too."

"What are you going to do?"

"What advent I going to do about what?"

"What are you going to do about Krista?"

"I told you. I'm taking her with myself. She can move while we're there."

"Don't do it, Candace, don't, it's a nowhere job."

"I wish I wasn't."

"Don't do it!"

"Shhhh. You'll awake Krista."

A swan slipped alongy the slimeway outside. It clippled around the gassing mounds of trash before it evaporated sunk the blizzard pipes.

"It's not a shiny swan," Krista murmured. It's a sad swan.

"Antiway, what's for morningthing, here?" came Candace's voice, waybelow.

"Cheese sandwiches!" rejoiced Charles.

"I've got to go get ready," Candace breathed.

A door widened.

A door crashed.

All of Krista's TV splashes pulledto around the cozy cot. Spec of them were her mamamas' plumped toys she moved with eternily they got over to look Charles. Spec of them were Charles' tomes and drawing skeletons and other kings-and-things. Krista didn't look that they weren't as happy or tender as her other toys. That's climbing she mottled them in her brain for her other toys. That's the way it typically played. A grimy plumped creature became a Monster Ruler. A redscraped paperholder became her bestest gray flier. Zata smashed-to-a-crashed machine keything moofed a diver. Forma simple thing haya notted mottle kicked forma ickick stacks forn splicing outtere, fie haya could push forma downwater go down. Unto K-Baby, zat was fishy and lighty outside. Umpa, Umpa, haya could alwaysy ask formabove.

30 <251-WORD STORIES IN 30 DAYS

Originally published on connorcoyne.com

(April 2011)

#1: TOO FAST

He leapt out of bed before the alarm started ringing. As the first static chirp sheared the blanket bedroom air, both feet hit the floor. It had been too long. Friday night? It was a sacred time, when he forgot the strain of glowing computer screens, the dryness of papers for clients to sign, 1040s, 1099s, bitter boredom. He'd almost recovered from last Friday's hangover. Today would be even more magnificent.

Before the alarm had chirped ten times, he'd exchanged his sweaty briefs for neon blue boxers, a white wife-beater, a bevy of gold chains, some thick sunglasses, and sandals. He started to feel a pulling-apart, an intergalactic inflation, but he wrote this off as the mixed effect of adrenaline and caffeine. And speaking of caffeine... before the alarm had chirped sixteen times he'd made it to the kitchen and downed a mug of cold coffee and a shot of Bombay Sapphire.

Now the static swept across his skin, as if the circulation had been cut off everywhere. I feel bright and real! he thought, and before the alarm had chirped twenty times he had washed his face, slammed the door, and backed the black Fiero down the driveway. Electrical and now nuclear forces surged through his body. Tonight he'd hit twenty-one bars, dance at forty clubs, have seven one-night stands. He could taste the frisson in the air!

But he was moving too fast.

And all of the atoms in his body separated and scattered to the wind.

#2: THE CONVERSATION

Tracey filled her order at Panda Express and crossed the food court to the small round table. She sat down across from Margaret and scooped a forkful of rice into her mouth.

"Is it good?" Margaret asked.

"It's not bad."

"Glad to hear it."

"So how have you been?"

"Oh, not bad." Margaret scratched her head. "I've been spending a lot of time with Tim lately."

"Oh..." Awkward pause. "Is he –"

"Yeah, I know. It's a little strange. He's a nice guy, but there's just something off about him."

"Something?"

"Okay, you're right, I mean, a lot of things are off about him. I just don't think it should hide the fact that he's a basically decent human being."

"I guess. As long as there aren't any chopped up bodies in his basement."

"He has that lazy eye..."

"It never feels like he's looking at you!"

"It's like he looks right past you..."

"Right through you!"

"The guy can't dress at all."

"I know! Mismatched socks. Plaid shirt with polka dot pants."

"He smells weird. I don't think he does his laundry very often."

"I don't think he's gotten his hair cut in years!"

"I don't think he even brushes his teeth!"

"Stop it you guys!" I said. "If you're just going to say mean things about me then don't invite me along at all!"

#3: MADONNA

She was the least self-defined thing in the world. Practically nothing that had happened with her had been under her control. Once upon a time, she had been a coral swaying in the cradling arms of the tender ocean. After her death, she had settled, dried, became stiff and compressed. Then, for a long time — hundreds of millions of years — her calcium carbonate skeleton had been heated and crushed at a depth far from any living thing. She had emerged one day, and men with saws and chisels cut her free and sliced her up. Now she stood in rain and snow before the stone steps of Immaculate Conception Church. It wouldn't be long at all, all things considered, before the wind wore her down into something new again. But she wasn't self-defined and she didn't control it for a moment.

Sometimes, the boys and girls from the school next door would hide behind the trees and kiss within her view, and this filled her with longing. Sometimes, drunks would kick over garbage cans or graffiti up the playground, and this filled her with futile anger. But sometimes… sometimes…

Sometimes, an old woman in a shawl or an old man in black would step out through the heavy oak doors of the church, sit down beside her, and mutter some words. They'd stop halfway through their prayer, and stare out into space, feeling broken, worn-down, blown about. "I know exactly how you feel," she thought.

#4: ZEIT TODAY, ZILCH TOMORROW

(Inspired by the song "Friday," by Rebecca Black)
A performance of this piece may be viewed at
http://tinyurl.com/zeittodayzilchtomorrow

I sound vowel sounds.

Ages ante-meridian I bestir myself to motion.
I won't decay. This is my anti-apotheosis.
In hyperbolic planes, in the fruit of the earth,
time is relatively absolute for all
and I must partake of such motion.
There is hope to commune.

Before, behind, resolve. Recline?

It is the zeitgeist. Sink this zeitgeist. What is next? Another zeitgeist.
And so, in Dionysian moments of opulent ecstasy we lean into the next now.
Approaching the meridian in abridged vectors,
apprehending festal vestals
I identify and we claim,
a hemisphere affiliation. We've claimed
your convictions, unimpeachable.

Before, behind, resolve. Recline?

It is the zeitgeist. Sink this zeitgeist. What is next? Another zeitgeist.
Catharsis. Affirm catharsis. Elide form, evoke entropy, and lean into the next now.

Before this zeitgeist came another. But today is the day's zeitgeist. A sphere bridges two dimensions. And yet is ours.

After this zeitgeist, another. And then, yet another. But I prefer this set. This group. A meaning? They occlude?

>>> relaxed avant garde

>>> or perhaps the ages' guard

>>> I describe the boulevard

>>> and cautious lines discard

>>> another bestarred

>>> to seek out the school yard

>>> a crystal clock, my voice a shard

>>> This is today's temporal interlard

Dionysian ecstasy. Lean catharsis. You can't learn catharsis. Embrace catharsis. Embrace the zeitgeist.

We lean into the next now.

#5: SUGARBOY AND DEATH FISH

(Concept suggested by Sumara.)

I survey the playroom. The tragic sunlight makes a rectangle on the floor. The radiator's on cuz it's March. A cloud covers the sun. I look out the window. Yes just as I suspected it is a PURPLE cloud. And that means that Poison Potion has been put in the bottom of the POWER PLANT. It's going to KILL people! Who did it? I know who did it. DEATH FISH! did it. (DeathFish! is like a bad guy only like a fish with feet and goggles too.) Well that's okay, because I, Sugarboy, can do what it takes to stop it from happening. I have EVER ENERGY! and my CANDY OF INVISIBILITY! that will make me sneak up on Death Fish! from behind and bop him on the head so he falls down. Then I can turn the power plant into reverse and it sucks the Poison Potion back in. But there's too much. It builds and builds. Blowie!!! Oh, it's everywhere, the Poison covering Death Fish! like acid.

"I'm mellllltiiiiing!" he screams.

"Until next time Death Fish!" I say.

That's how I'll save the day. I'll do it right now. I'm going out the door. No you can't stop me. But maybe I'll just sit down for a minute first. Maybe I'll just lie here and figure out the other parts of the PLAN. You have to have a PLAN; a good PLAN! Ow! Phew, I feel SLEEPY!

#6: THE BEAR, OR, I WROTE THIS STORY IN 15 SECONDS FLAT

The bear walked out of the woods carrying a bear bell in its jaws.

#X: WHAT A LOOKER

(This story did not count toward the thirty because it was over 250 words.)

(Concept suggested by Michael.)

It's been fifteen minutes.

This has happened before. Like a player piano that gets halfway through a sweet old tune and then someone kicks on the mute, well, this is how it goes:

"Btw, can you send me a picture? I want to know you when I see you!"

He's gotten good at delaying this moment. His digital camera is broken (of course) and he doesn't really like the intrusiveness of the internet (naturally). He's honest, but vague: "I don't think anyone would really consider me to be a 'looker.'" He doesn't fall into that hypocritical trap of asking the ex-homecoming queen. He's not interested, to be honest. He's allowed to be a little discriminating, right? He maneuvers around the question. He sets up a time and a date. Then, when it's past the "point of no return," he finally sends a picture. What could go wrong? Nothing! Except this is the third time he's been stood up.

It's been thirty minutes, so he studies the menu again. He doesn't understand why those mozzarella sticks are almost as expensive as the olive burger. Maybe he'll go ahead and order them both. After all, it looks like he's eating for two. He sees the shadow of his waitress on the table and hears her say something about his order, his night, and would he like some more coffee?

"Sure," he says, and orders dinner. He gets the mozzarella sticks. And the olive burger. And why not, the key lime pie. The waitress sighs and returns to the kitchen. She blinks in the bright fluorescent glare, and puts the order up.

"How'd it go?" asks the cook.

"He didn't seem to be paying attention," she says. "Anyway, I'm not exactly a 'looker,' right?"

#7: IN THE ABSENCE OF EVIDENCE

The sun rose. It slanted against the walls at an almost horizontal angle. The murderer sat up in bed. It had happened the night before. He still couldn't believe he had gone through with it. He got up, shaved, brushed his teeth, ate breakfast. Nervous about trace evidence he might have left behind, he went back over each moment. He had ground up sleeping pills in the victim's sugar dish months earlier. He had air tight alibis for weeks and weeks. It was a meticulous effort. The elderly victim had been in poor health. There were any number of likely causes of death, and the murderer doubted the next of kin would request an autopsy. The murderer stood to gain nothing obvious by the death; it had been a simple act of revenge in return for a slight many decades earlier. The murder had shared his feelings with nobody, so he didn't expect to be suspected. Still, he felt a nagging uncertainty.

He went outside, got in his car, and started the daily trip downtown. The traffic tightened around him; rush hour is hell. The sun went behind a cloud, and he started to feel the eyes watching him. The man in the pickup behind him. The woman walking her dog. The children in the playground. The murderer looked down the long freeway, and knew that in every car and on every sidewalk, everyone was thinking of him at that very moment. Condemning him and the crime he had committed.

#8: THE MINNIE AND HER SISTERS

Of all of the crazy conspiracies I've investigated, this one seems the least likely. Sure, I'm a nut for the things, but even among conspiracy theorists, there a hierarchy of plausibility. The man on the grassy knoll has always seemed reasonable to me. Area 51, far less plausible. And then there's the fabrication of the 1969 moon landing, which is an embarrassment to conspiracy theorists as far as I'm concerned.

I've always figured that the vast majority of theories are bogus, but if just one of them proves right, and I provide the big reveal, then my future fame and career are assured. But of all the plots and webs I've tried to uncover, this one always struck me as bizarre. Still, here I am, rolling down an unmarked dirt road in Esmeralda County, Nevada. I pull up at a rocky outcropping with an inconspicuous hole going down into the ground. I lower myself in. My feet touch down on a smooth metal surface. I shoot my flashlight beam the length of the hull, to a place where 'THE MINNIE' is painted in back letters. It's a yacht. In 1983, The Minnie vanished less than two days after sailing due east from Fort Lauderdale. I take a picture.

I clamber down off the hull and wander deeper into the cave. Already the light beam plays off the distant edges of dozens and dozens of ships and airplanes, and who knows how many skeletons. Fame and fortune, here I come!

#9: PATIENCE IS THE COMPANION OF WISDOM

"Peace be with you," the churchgoers say en masse, and they smile with beneficence through the conclusion of the Agnus Dei. The chalice is full. The host has been blessed. Now the moment has come.

A small old woman in the centermost seat of the front row creaks to her feet behind her walker. It is a scene that a single frame of film might have caught, because the next moment she is down, crushed by a linebacker of a man who has just rushed up from halfway back. The bent and shattered walker pokes up like syringes of the medicine the old woman won't be needing anymore.

But now the linebacker is having trouble of his own, for a cluster of middle-aged women and bejeaned high schoolers slowly asphyxiate him as they clamber over, under, and around him. The pews are empty and silent for a moment, except for the nonbelievers and unrepentent divorcees who are now being crushed as the seats topple over, front to back, like a row of oaken dominoes. The spray of sweat and vitae gives the lighting a reddish quality more commonly associated with a Who concert. The priest looks serenely on as the piles grow deeper and deeper, the cries from the bottom grow feebler and feebler. At last the ministers of the sacrament succumb, every last one, and all is silent in the church.

The body and blood of the Lord looks out upon the blood and bodies of the congregants

#10: ANGELO'S MEDITATION #1

(Concept suggested by Colin.)

There is nothing to her more serious than the Chinese Masters. Nothing more precise than their careful craft. They were from far away and spoke a language she does not know. They lived long ago and did not know each other. They wrote moral and social codes, planted gardens and then painted them, waged war according to an exquisite plan, and built a land that has never died. Never. It is the precision and care in their art that sustained them.

She doesn't consider herself to be particularly serious. There is nothing precise in the lines of the ball-point pen shamrock tattoo. It was a lack of care that led to the two children who are at home sleeping right now. The night grows long and fierce, and she laughs away as much of it as she can.

Still, she calls upon the Masters in the early hours of the morning, when they inspire her in the most perilous tasks. The restaurant is a coney island. A coney is a Koegel Vienna hot dog covered in a meat sauce, drenched with mustard, with onions piled on. They are meant to be served on a plate, not handed out through a cracked window at 4 AM, and across a huge space into the dark mouth of a waiting car. Every time there is a risk of accident, of slipping, of scattering, of ruination. But she has gotten good at this, calling upon her muses and the serenity of a still hour.

#11: ANGELO'S MEDITATION #2

Death followed him from a very young age.

They first glimpsed each other in the early 80s, when he was walking back home to his house on Devil's Lake. Someone started shooting, and a stray bullet missed his head by about a foot.

Out of work a decade later, he joined the Army and was promptly shipped off to Iraq. That time, he took a bullet in the leg, which probably kept him from stepping on the landmine that got the guy to his side.

When he got home, things settled down for a bit. He got a job at Angelo's Coney Island and worked with dignity even though his coworkers walked with bile and muttered racist epithets under their breath. He was a favorite among the customers. His smiles were never strained, but frank, and he seemed made for the night shift, still on-stride as the sun came up. It wasn't a paradise, no, not by a long shot, but it was a pause. A draw your breath in deep and let it out still and smooth. Outside Angelo's in the midnight and summer, you heard crickets.

Death finally caught up with him in the mid-2000s. No bullets. No landmines. A heart attack. It was instantaneous. Maybe he was genetically predisposed. Or maybe someone so wrapped in beatitudes is just the most provisional of guests in our world.

#12: ROCKING THE BOAT

The convicts rejoiced. Things couldn't have gone any better. They had burrowed their way out of the penitentiary before the clock struck midnight, and they figured that bought them at least a few hours before their absence was noticed. They'd made it down to the pier, and as they ran it rained hard. Soon the snow was all gone along with their footprints. They had made it to the river in record time and stole a rowboat which would quickly whisk them as far as Kalamazoo.

"Don't let those waves rock us too much," said the first convict.

"Why not?" asked the second. "I feel free."

"If it rocks, we might sink and drown."

"It doesn't matter. Our existence is strictly provisional, and perhaps even the fabrication of a greater mind than ours."

#13: JANUARY IS JANUARY

(Concept suggested by Ms. Sharrow.)

January is January. Unless you live in Rio. If you live in Rio, then January is July. It is so July that the residents respond to the weather as if it actually was July. Their July is their January, although not nearly as January as Duluth's January. Duluth's January was very January, as Richard could plainly see from his desk on the first floor of the North Shore Bank of Commerce. It had less to do with the slight covering of snow and more to do with the way the few pedestrians clenched their jackets in steel-strong fists and ducked their heads into the cold to blunt the wind.

But in Rio today, there would be none of this. Richard gave a slight nod, and shuffled the discards into a neat stack. He stood to take them to the shredder. In Rio, right now, this very moment, the salsa dancers were in practice for their marvelous carnaval. They dressed up in bright yellows and reds and wound their way to the schools through the drab gray favelas. And when they got there, oh, how the music would shake from the speakers like a herd of tapirs on the run before a storm. The music would shake and the dancers would dance and Richard took a leap in the air.

His hand slipped and papers fell all over the place.

"This floor is too slick!" he barked. "Someone could get killed."

#14: ABORTED HARRY POTTER FAN FICTION #1

With a quick tick of his head, Franklin Pierce blew the hair from his face. His boyish face was lit up with malevolent delight. "Avada Kedavra!" he screamed, followed by a burst of green light from the sugar maple wand.

Winfield Scott howled and fell on his face, instantly dead.

Okay this story sucks, time to move on

#15: EASTER EGG

1. Buy a DVD

2. Scan the beach with metal detector until you have obtained multiple pieces of colored glass.

3. Devise a cypher.

4. Start a social networking meme.

5. Read the Bible.

6. Make a JPop and Electroclash compilation.

7. Salvage metal scrap from dumpsters and junk yards (do not lift it illegally from peoples' houses).

8. Write a poem.

9. Eat a pomegranate.

10. Read the Upanishad.

11. Out Oulipo Oulipo.

12. Fuse glass pieces to firm metal pieces to make an artistically meaningful lampshade.

13. Melt wax onto recycled newsprint so that letters inscribe your poem in code.

14. Read the phone book.

15. Build a circuit board such that electrical resistance builds up considerable quantities of heat.

16. Meet the surviving descendents of Lyndon Baines Johnson for coffee and significant conversation.

17. Insert and coil wiring into a column fitted with a socket and light bulb. Attach lampshade to make a lovely and full-functioning lamp.

18. Collate.

19. Read your poem by the light of the lamp.

20. Internet search your DVD and access all available Easter Eggs.

#16: THROTTLE

Integrity wounds. It is the thing that prompts us to take high stake gambles. Therefore, those who risk much must have integrity. Observation tells us that this is not so. There are many for whom the nudge of hunger is fully sufficient. And so when Samson motored his bike down the street at great speed, full throttle daring the lights to change their color. He believes, personally, in his heart, that there is some enduring principle at work, and that something will be lost – something of character and soul – if he stops at any of the three lights between himself and the viaduct. And while he isn't hit or flipped or killed, he is not faster than the speed of light, and the drive of the sedan that interrupts his red with the screech of brakes assumes he's an arrogant fool gambling with his own and others' lives

#17: WAVES AND SHADOWS

He's terrified of waves, which is a real shame because they've been in the news a lot lately... in recent years, that is. In 2004 the day after Christmas was spoiled when a tsunami hit southeast Asia, and while he didn't know anyone from that part of the world, he shook in the shadows of his bedtime bedroom imagining an explosion of water that shears through tree trunks and scatters humans like kindling. He was grateful for his second story bedroom, but after Katrina, the next year, when hundreds of human bodies were found in attics and on roofs, he was't so sure. He knew that these people knew about the power of water; perhaps they did not respect it enough.

And then Japan, a nation that had wrestled with such things for centuries and knew well the might and majesty and deadly terror of fast water. He saw actual footage, not so much an explosion of water as a rapid surge that rose and rose, higher and higher. He trembled through those night time shadows. He imagined running into the lake at a young age and hitting the sinkhole and the waves – small waves, timid and inoffensive waves – closing over his head with a non-negotiable finality. The nighttime shadows reminded him of the waves. Now, he lives in New Mexico. But he is still afraid. Three-quarters of the world is covered in water, and maybe that is greedy for the rest.

#18: SOMETHING ISN'T RIGHT HERE

Daphne dances.

She doesn't like it, strictly.

There's something wrong with this DJ.

She can't put her finger on the problem, exactly. He seems to have the genres set appropriately and in balance. He's nice in that he weaves in the artsy stuff without clearing the dance floor. A glitch in the drum and bass. He can't seem to keep his decades straight, but in this case, it's a good thing. The club is performing well, too. Too much fog seems like a cheap stage effect; here it just curls around the feet, almost invisible, an illusion of incense since the club went smoke free. The lights aren't strobes; they don't beat down on you, but they do sear with the kind of intensity typically reserved for a desert sun. She is certainly sweating enough to feel like the night was worthwhile, but something is wrong here. Something doesn't quite add up. Something is lodged in the back of her brain. There is something wrong with this DJ.

Is it the Ray-Ban sunglasses that look like he fished them up off the floor after some hipster stepped on them?

Is it the corduroy pants that don't really go with his plaid shirt (which looks way too hot, for real).

Or maybe it's the third arm that extends from the middle of his chest and helps him spin the vinyl.

#19: NONE TOO GENTLE

Sitting on the lawn. Gentle branches overhead. Gentle leaves. (How can leaves be gentle?) (They're the ones with the smooth edging, no sawtooth fronds, so that if by chance that they are clipped off in a rough wind, there is virtually no risk of them cutting up against your skin.) Gentle wind. But that jazz isn't gentle that blasts back over the audience of the forest preserve. That jazz band up on that chopped up white pine stage isn't gentle as they squeal discordantly across themselves and leave a tangle of sound and noise in the ears and brains of the fifty odd-listeners. No, they ignite that place like an atomic bomb and all those people have their hair blown back by the sound, and their shadows become tattoos on the gentle green grass.

#20: VLADIMIR NABOKOV

Vladimir Nabokov woke up one morning and found himself in a big bedroom without any ornamentation except for a large bed of fused wrought iron and a single framed painting on the wall. He climbed out of bed and stepped barefoot, nightgown swooshing around his legs, up to the painting. On closer inspection he realized that it was actually a photograph, blurred like the ink had been streaked by wet fingers against wet photo paper. He strained to recognize the features of the man there, a man wearing a short old-fashioned hat – not quite a fedora – with a wry, a cynical, a vaguely superior smile. The man there, streaked as he was, would not interview without seeing questions in advance. He liked butterflies a little bit too much, and had little nice to say about communism. And that was the moment when Vladimir realized that he was just a character in someone else's story.

"Son of a bitch!" he swore, and knew this was uncharacteristic.

How utterly ironic.

#21: MARTIAN SEXCAPADE

Ernest, a cryogenically frozen astronaut, was excited to be the first human being recruited to study the experience of sex on Mars. While extensive experiments had been performed on scientists in Earth orbit and on the moon, NASA had to be thorough in anything and everything, and the gravitational field of Mars (and the effect of trace amounts of atmospheric iron oxide suit permeation) was an unknown quantity. So they had selected Ernest to test out sex with several partners. They had queried him extensively on his preferences (which ranged from white to black, buxom to flat, raven-headed to blonde) and on his sexual preferences (which were even more inclusive and varied) and promised that all of his desires would be satisfied so long as he submitted his data. It was certainly the best gig he had ever gotten. The whole trip – two-and-a-half years – he dreamt all sorts of kinky dreams involving whipped cream and honey and riding crops and bunny outfits and jumping so so so high in the air.

If the dreams were this delicious, he thought, what would the reality be like?

When the ship touched down, the computer thawed him and his partners. Trembling with excitement he approached the first one's chamber. He knocked. No reply. She must be shy! he thought with delight. Almost bursting with excitement, he reached out and pushed the door open. On the floor he saw a modest bicycle pump and a wrinkled flesh-colored plastic doll.

#22: UNDER THE BLUE LINE

The student revolutionary hung her head. Now that MTV had opened a house for *The Real World* in her favorite Marxy neighborhood, the process of gentrification seemed complete. It was exotic, really, to most of the world, this feeling she felt, but it isn't giving fair credit to say that she felt it naively. She had thought this to be a fertile recruiting ground, under the Blue Line, under the station, whatever was lost, whatever had been spent here in the midst of capitalist splendor: it was still a place where the smell of cheap newsprint and tamales rode the streets in rich and interweaving flavors. These were people to be recruited. But Viacom told her what she already knew, secretly. This neighborhood was already lost. It had been lost from the beginning. It wasn't old bourgeois, but it was something new and equally contradictory. It called her attention to herself; the economic contradictions in her own history. But she didn't want to give up. She believed this was really, really, really, really, really, really important. She urgently needed to be part of the solution, not one in the deck of problems.

Time to buy some tamales for a quick break, a burst of energy.

Time to ride the Blue Line one stop further on.

#23: IOTA

Iota, Louisiana is somewhere out in the swamps between New Orleans and Houston. It is a speck, unknown, and by custom, Cajun, cajoling, bizarre, it is not generally known by outsiders. This is where Andrew went to escape February and high school. Back in Cleveland, February had pursued him from year to year, the death dirge of winter, long before spring became a real thing, impartially vindictive, objectively callous, cruel, careful, ruthless, death and death. He thought he would escape it in Louisiana. And high school pursued him. Without a college degree, without any jobs in his burnt out town, he felt stuck in the moment of the closest success he had ever known; honor roll grades and appreciative teachers, and girls that admired him even if they did not love him.

Iota was meant to be an escape. It wasn't long before he realized that the bayou has all kinds of death he didn't know and wouldn't have recognized through his rust belt eyes. Death lay just beneath the brackish surface, and more creatures lived a short life here. If his high school moments seemed futile, they were something next to these strange and inaccessible accents.

So he spent summer nights in his hammock and dreamed about Cleveland and February, and drank himself asleep.

#24: THE RHYTHM METHOD

Catholic Roulette.

#25: TWO MINUTES TO MIDNIGHT

The writer became increasingly stressed out. Mephistopheles was standing in the corner and he knew that he was two minutes away from getting another soul on his ledger.

#26: BOOM!

A bomb went off.

That's okay. It was just a P-Funk album.

Everyone wiped the sweat off their brows and proceeded to get down.

It was a good night.

#27: AS GOOD AS GOLD

When King Midas announced his intention to run for the Republican Presidential nomination, everyone assumed it was a publicity stunt. After all, he had a variety of products, venues, and enterprises, and the grand sum of everything considered together was somewhere close to breaking even. That's why Midas coveted gold.

He surprised the world twice.

He surprised them first when he accepted the challenge and won the nomination and, incredibly, won the actual election.

He also surprised them the very next day, when he developed the remarkable power to transform anything he touched into gold. But since this is the world we live in and not a Greek myth, we know that everything is connected by a tight web of matter and energy, light and dark. And so, in less than a blink, a second, and without recognition, the whole universe turned to gold. It was an unexpected end to an extraordinary few billion years.

#28: THE BURN

The insult burned so bad he had to have a whole bowl of soup to soothe his flayed tongue. His victim, on the other hand, had to cover himself in aloe vera. It was a pretty sore day for both of them, and their friendship never fully recovered.

#29: SOMETHING ISN'T RIGHT HERE, PART 2

Tyrone thinks there isn't something right about this DJ, with his Ray-Ban sunglasses, his corduroys, his nonchalance… but what could it be? As Tyrone tries to decipher the puzzle, he scratches his head with two of his tentacles while using the rest to light cigarettes and order drinks for the many women surrounding him.

#30: TWENTY-THREE MINUTES AFTER MIDNIGHT

The writer didn't even have the meager pride of Dr. Faust's reckless ambition. Instead, procrastination had been the culprit this time. Procrastination… and a demanding and needy child! Never a man to breach a contract, Mephistopheles gave the child her bottle as promised, and whisked the writer away to the lake of fire. There, twenty-three minutes is longer than an eternity.

PLACES I'D LIKE TO LIVE BEFORE I DIE: THE FINAL EDITION

An essay, originally published on connorcoyne.com

(27 December 2012)

Every year or so, I've compiled a list of "places I'd like to live before I die." It isn't a particularly realistic bucket list... if you have to know a place in order to have lived there, I've lived in both Flint and Chicago for more than a decade, and I still make unexpected discoveries about both of these places. Each list gets longer than the last, and yet they never seem to change much otherwise.

Last year I decided to try a different strategy: since the list is idealized to begin with, I might as well make it "ideal" (and in that sense, finish it "for good"). Then instead of rewriting the list in the future, I could learn more about the locations on it. So I really dug in, reading a bit about every country, and locations within each country, and at last the list started to change, as my misconceptions and the popular attention each selection had been given melted away. It's been very educational. I built the list up to a total of 575 entries, and then ruthlessly slashed it down to 100.

Here are the rules I've followed in my final selection:

1. "Living" in a place requires enough time to settle into a routine and to make some cultural discoveries hidden or obscured during shorter visits. I felt like I was approaching, if not achieving, this goal, when I spent one month in Iași, Romania in 2001. I've settled on the more-or-less arbitrary duration of three months.

2. The list is subjective... it isn't meant to be objective. Therefore, the list prefers my own country (the U.S.A.) in some instances, while also being biased towards places where friends have lived, of which I already have some knowledge and experience, or which have simply excited my curiosity for a long time.

3. Every place I have already lived is automatically included on the list.

4. Safety is not an issue. In real life, if I was going to live in Baghdad or the McMurdo Station, my safety and sanity would be pressing concerns. Since this is an idealized list, I'm not worrying about them here.

5. Ditto expense. Money is not an issue.

6. Ditto language. Communication is perhaps an issue, but it is one to be embraced.

7. I did make invoke one pragmatic consideration... in some countries, I prefer cities or capitals that are centrally located with access to numerous points of interest. So, for example, Medan, Indonesia is not only chosen because it is an interesting city in its own right (it is) but also because it provides amenities and access to a larger area of Sumatra.

8. Since I've got 100 entries, all entries do not have to be all things. I've got room for urban entries and rural entries, developed entries and undeveloped entries, hot entries and cold entries, and Christian/Muslim/Jewish/Hindu/Buddhist/Etc. entries. And so on. In other words, 100 choices allows me build a list of broad diversity, and I have tried to do so.

Here's my bucket list of 100 Places to Live Before I Die:

PLACES I'VE ALREADY LIVED

1. FLINT, MICHIGAN, U.S.A.
2. FLUSHING, MICHIGAN, U.S.A.
3. FLUSHING TOWNSHIP, MICHIGAN, U.S.A.
4. CHICAGO, ILLINOIS, U.S.A.
5. BROOKLYN, NEW YORK, U.S.A.

PLACES I'D LIKE TO LIVE

6. ADAMSTOWN, PITCAIRN ISLANDS
7. ANSE LA RAYE, SAINT LUCIA
8. ARUSHA, TANZANIA
9. ATHENS, GREECE
10. BAGHDAD, IRAQ
11. BALYCHY, KYRGYZSTAN
12. BEIJING, CHINA
13. BEIRUT, LEBANON
14. BERLIN, GERMANY
15. BUCHAREST, ROMANIA
16. BUENOS AIRES, ARGENTINA
17. CAIRO, EGYPT
18. CAPE TOWN, SOUTH AFRICA

19. CLUJ, ROMANIA
20. COLOMBO, SRI LANKA
21. CONSTANTA, ROMANIA
22. CUZCO, PERU
23. DENVER, COLORADO, U.S.A.
24. DETROIT, MICHIGAN, U.S.A.
25. DHAKA, BANGLADESH
26. DUBLIN, IRELAND
27. GUILIN, CHINA
28. HAVANA, CUBA
29. HILO, HAWAII, U.S.A.
30. HO CHI MINH CITY, VIETNAM
31. HONG KONG, CHINA
32. IRKUTSK, RUSSIA
33. ISFARA, TAJIKISTAN
34. ISTANBUL, TURKEY
35. JACKSON, WYOMING, U.S.A.
36. JAKARTA, INDONESIA
37. JERUSALEM, ISRAEL
38. JUBA, SOUTH SUDAN
39. KOLKATA, INDIA
40. KOROR, PALAU
41. KYOTO, JAPAN
42. LAE, PAPUA NEW GUINEA
43. LAGOS, NIGERIA
44. LAHORE, PAKISTAN
45. LA PAZ, BOLIVIA
46. LHASA, TIBET (CHINA)
47. LJUBLJANA, SLOVENIA
48. LONDON, ENGLAND (U.K.)
49. LOS ANGELES, CALIFORNIA, U.S.A.
50. LUANG PRABANG, LAOS
51. LUSAKA, ZAMBIA
52. MAHEBOURG, MAURITIUS
53. MANAUS, BRAZIL
54. MARQUETTE, MICHIGAN, U.S.A.
55. MARRAKECH, MOROCCO
56. MATAGALPA, NICARAGUA
57. MC MURDO STATION, ANTARCTICA
58. MEDAN, INDONESIA
59. MELBOURNE, AUSTRALIA
60. MEMPHIS, TENNESSEE, U.S.A.
61. MEXICO CITY, MEXICO
62. MIAMI, FLORIDA, U.S.A.

63. MONROVIA, LIBERIA
64. MONTPELLIER, FRANCE
65. MOPTI, MALI
66. MOSCOW, RUSSIA
67. MUMBAI, INDIA
68. NAMPULA, MOZAMBIQUE
69. NAPLES, ITALY
70. NEW ORLEANS, LOUISIANA, U.S.A.
71. OSH, KYRGYZSTAN
72. PARIS, FRANCE
73. PHNOM PENH, CAMBODIA
74. PLACENCIA, BELIZE
75. PORT ELIZABETH, SOUTH AFRICA
76. PORTO, PORTUGAL
77. REYKJAVIK, ICELAND
78. RIO DE JANEIRO, BRAZIL
79. ST. PETERSBURG, RUSSIA
80. SAMARA, RUSSIA
81. SAMARKAND, UZBEKISTAN
82. SANA'A YEMEN
83. SAN FRANCISCO, CALIFORNIA, U.S.A.
84. SAPANTA, ROMANIA
85. SEATTLE, WASHINGTON, U.S.A.
86. SEOUL, SOUTH KOREA
87. SHANGHAI, CHINA
88. SIENA, ITALY
89. SRINAGAR, INDIA
90. STOCKHOLM, SWEDEN
91. SUVA, FIJI
92. TOKYO, JAPAN
93. VILNIUS, LITHUANIA
94. TIMBUNKE, PAPUA NEW GUINEA
95. VUKTYL, RUSSIA
96. WARSAW, POLAND
97. WASHINGTON, D.C., U.S.A.
98. YAKUTSK, RUSSIA
99. YELLOWKNIFE, NORTHWEST TERRITORIES, CANADA
100. ZACATECAS, MEXICO

MAXIMILIEN ROBESPIERRE ADDRESSES
HIS MIRROR ON THE MATTER
OF MICHIGAN GOVERNOR RICK SNYDER

Today is tedious.

But tomorrow could be calamity, cataclysms, earthquakes, comets, and degenerations!

I see my eyes. The clockmaker and the philosopher should get together, sit down to drink a bottle of wine, and discuss the mechanical implications of metaphysical interconnections. Science is part of the answer. Our eyes are lucid and spectral, shimmering, absorbing light and making meaning of it. Yet despite our observation of these facts, we often see too much in the aspect of our eyes. They are not portals to the searching brain, beating heart, throbbing soul. They are lenses, curved surfaces with balls and globes suspended to make meaning of light.

Yet science is not the only part of the answer. We are remiss if we reduce our eyes to mere receptacles. To be infused with light, to absorb it, to take it in and dispense its contents as facts, as information, as the characteristics of the streets and the gutters and rooftops and the angry people with their angry faces, this, this is reflected upon our souls. Reflected quite literally, in fact. Our thoughts move in our brain which is fed by our blood, and our blood moves back and forth between our brain and our eyes. How appropriate, then, that our eyes have rings, rungs, gears even, our irises, our pupils, wheels interlocking fine threads of color, suspended on an open face, a face that takes a simple shape or a burst of light or color and makes it meaningful.

So yes: I think our philosopher and clockmaker should get together over wine and discuss this matter thoroughly. Conversation is more than their right; it is their responsibility.

Today is tired.

I hope that tomorrow will be the most dire, the most expansive calamity. I have been selected to serve, to attend. Tomorrow the Constituent Assembly will meet again. The nobles are getting restless. They understand that their freewheeling peregrinations are drawing to a close. They're not invested in present prosperity but future survival. As for the king; he doesn't even know what is happening. He still imagines that this is a farce, a court satire, a particularly expensive lost or stolen diamond necklace. And so, the moderates grin like devils. They believe that tradition draws us back toward the center. Even my friends and allies misread the tea leaves. They expect that they'll be dragged away, heels in the dust and snow, leaving nothing but temporary dirty tracks to remind others of where we tried to travel.

They are, in fact, all wrong.

The extent of our enemies' audacities can only affect to make conspicuous their pernicious distance from the truth. The truth and the future are both nearer than they think. Already, when I put my ears to the windows, hear the churn of wagon wheels, the stomping of angry people in their cottages, the regular dripping of rainwater into the gutters, the gutters into the river... there is a monstrous hungry impatience here. It has recognized me, this impatience. It has endowed me with authority. Recognition will take the reins.

And so I recognize: Tomorrow I'll motion again for the abolition of capital punishment. It's another stone, and already many roll. The avengers, the self-righteous, the self-informed and self-assured; they're all murderers. It may be that they themselves deserve death and they argue this fact through the whiteness of their wigs and the pallor of their powdered faces. They are fortunate, then, that the voice of true Enlightenment does not call for earned blood, the sundering of eyes and mind, but only for resolution, respect, and reason. I believe this. We need this. When I listen to the wheels in the river, eddies and strong currents, when I close my eyes and listen to their ticking, I ache for the future.

I'll attend with them for a little while longer. I'll put on my own wig. I'll powder my own face. I'll go out into the assembly as their friend, their adviser, the voice of their future, their Maximilien. After all, they chose me, and they will follow me wherever I choose to lead them. And when I stand atop that mountain, they will see my eyes.

Gears, rungs, and wheels.

Movement.

Movement tomorrow.

IN FLINT

Originally published in Flint Broadside, #17 (2011)

In Flint, it is no longer necessary to buy power from Detroit. Flint electrifies itself on methane deposits that have seeped into the water supply of Lakes Michigan, Huron, and St. Clair. As long as the regional population remains stable and continues to create rancid garbage at a fixed rate, the supply of methane is unending and inexhaustible. Granular methane trickles into lake water from the big cities and is evenly circulated by Gallium Convectionizers placed evenly throughout the lakes at a depth of fifty feet. Vorpal Jets arrayed midway between each Convectionizer burn the methane current as it accumulates, and rubber-encased titanium cables snake onto the shore and spiderweb their way back toward Genesee County. Their sinuous routes are camouflaged so that they cannot be sabotaged by jealous rival cities. Unfortunately, there is a side effect. In order to maintain the necessary convection to transport methane, the heaters increase the temperature of the lakes by an average of eight degrees, resulting in a higher rate of evaporation. This fuels a Category Five Temperate Cyclone that drizzles and blizzards throughout the year. Eventually this system will transform the entire Great Lakes region into a polluted marsh and will drive away its people, the source of Flint's power. When that day arrives, we must have prepared an alternative.

In Flint, whenever a homicide is reported, we plant one million perennial flowers within a mile radius of the crime. The city has budgeted for vandalism and inclement weather; every destroyed flower is replaced at the end of the year. The crime rate has dropped by 87%, and Flint is the new home of the American Horticultural Society. Holland can eat its heart out.

In Flint, whenever one's virginity is declared "lost," the whole city celebrates with fireworks to illuminate the inky night of the soul and a sequined and bemasked parade sets forth in search of missing purity. No confirmation of the deed is required, only a public declaration. An unanticipated effect is that a numbers of citizens have become "born-again virgins" only to proclaim their multiple deflowerings.

In Flint, the citizens have taken to hibernating in the winter. They cannot literally hibernate, being humans without the proper metabolic machinery, but they simulate the effect as best they can. From September to

November, residents hurry about the North End Botanical Garden, collecting nuts and seeds and salami. They curl up in nests that they construct amid the wood paneling of their basements and spend the next five months eating Little Debbies, sleeping, and watching VHS tapes of the Fraggles. Some won't emerge until mid-May.

In Flint, there is no need for water purification. Each house comes with its own Welwitschia.

In Flint, the MTA buses have all been scrapped for public art projects involving murals and vertical walls of aluminum, covered with rubber and painted with dyed egg yolks. In practice, it is difficult to distinguish artistic eggings from those perpetrated by angry former commuters.

In Flint, a new public transit system involves reactivated factories across town. Smokestacks have been struck into the earth at various angles, and engineers calculate each rider's mass and aerodynamic potential. Commuters strap into parachutes, and pay one dollar to be pneumatically cannonballed at their destinations.

In Flint, a new public transit system involves elevated train stations arrayed like a clock. Shuttles depart from the terminus downtown (which is not the MTA building but the fully-restored Capitol Theatre). Shuttles move back and forth from the center along two hands which each rotate at a rate of one revolution per hour and one per day. These rates of revolution are maintained by a train of cement mixers which pull the far removed ends of the track along a concrete highway circumscribing the city at an exact distance of eight miles from the Capitol. Commuters select the arm of their choice and stand at the windows as the shuttles move outward. When they spy their destination, they leap from the moving cars, and wrap their arms around brass poles placed for their convenience. They slide down to the streets below.

In Flint, it is no longer necessary to buy power from Detroit. Flint electrifies itself on methane deposits that have seeped into the water supply of Lakes Michigan, Huron, and St. Clair. Unfortunately, there is a side effect. In order to prevent the sublimation of granular methane, the lakes must maintain an ice-cover year round. To this end, Flint's factories have been reactivated as incinerators producing enough soot to produce a tropospheric dust cover, effectively lowering the temperature in the region to a permanent twelve degrees, and encouraging a stable blocking front to permanently float over the state. Eventually this will transform the entire Great Lakes region into an arctic desert and will probably drive away its people, the source of Flint's power. When that day arrives, we must have prepared an alternative.

Various cafes have promised free coffee/beer/tea/tattoos/puppies for life to anyone who maintains a Civic Park address. The neighborhood's population has tripled in two months.

Excerpt from
URBANTASM

A novel in development since July 1995

In the flushest years at Ellis Island, as overladen ships waked the gray waves and passed into New York Harbor, small groups of Greeks clustered at the prows and pointed at the broad banks of twinkling lights in the distance.

"Είναι ότι η New York?" they'd ask a deckhand or whoever happened to be standing nearby.

"Ya," he'd reply. "That's Coney Island."

"Coney Island," the emigrants repeated in awe, leaning out over the churning ocean to get a better look at their new home. It was sparkling bright, shimmering, these ethereal, auroral sparks in the morning twilight, murmured invitations from the Cyclone, the Wonder Wheel, to taste the delights of the Boardwalk, of Luna Park, Steeplechase, Dreamland, and rapture on off of the Parachute Drop. The lights preceded the long queues, the dirty work, the discrimination against these Orthodox Christians with their swinging censers and their bearded priests. In the hard years to come the emigrants always held that first vision of Coney Island in their memories, because it was their first, unsullied glimpse of the Americas, and it had seemed to confirm the promise of a better life here. That's why, days, or weeks, or years later, having saved up scraps from their factory jobs, or having snuck small fortunes overseas, sewn into their threadbare jackets, when they opened hot dog stands in the industrial cities of southeast Michigan, they called them "Coney Islands."

That's the story I was told growing up. Like so many of our New World origin stories, it's pretty much bullshit. The immigrants called their wieners "coney islands" because they bought them at Coney Island, and the local Chamber of Commerce banned the words "hot dog" because they figured stupid immigrants might think their wieners were made from actual dogs.

But when the stupid immigrants arrived in Michigan and started selling their own coney islands in the nineteen teens, they wisely decided to improve their product. The American hot dogs had little in common with the Old World Würstl, freshly butchered and ground and encased. Thus began a long process of prayer and experimentation, roots plucked from tiny backyard gardens, cattle slaughtered at the altar, with providential navigation toward the apotheosis of the hot dog.

The core of this creation was the wiener itself, and from 1914 these were produced under arcane secrecy by the Richard Goerlich Bavarian Encased Meats Company, later known simply as "Goerlich's." Perhaps as a nod to the melting pot that threw the German Lutherans in with the Balkanites, a Goerlich was made out of many animals. A puree of pork and beef with secret spices were pressed together in a lambskin casing, tied off and smoked over a hardwood grill. The pork content meant that these viennas could be grilled for longer than other wieners without burning and shrinking. The spices were sweet and sour -- traces of mustard, sugar, vinegar, and salt. When you bit into a Goerlich, you felt the skin snap before your teeth sank into its soft inner flesh.

A Goerlich alone, however, was not enough to make the new coney. To turn a Goerlich into a coney, you had to top it with coney sauce, mustard, and onions, on a bun, on a hot plate with a hot cup of coffee on the side. To do it right, everything must be fresh. Even the mustard, the simplest ingredient, must taste as sharp as a paring knife and shine as bright as the sun. The Balkanites didn't just chop their onions into large, trapezoidal chunks. Onions were precision-cubed by calloused hands at half the speed of sound before being swept into oak barrels and sealed and chilled until called into use. Akawean Jewish and gentile bakeries supplied the buns, which the Balkanites steamed before setting them onto the bun-shaped waxed paper gracing the elliptical china plates. The thick china plates kept your food from burning your fingers. The thick china cups kept your coffee from cooling off.

I haven't described the sauce. I've saved the best for last. Finely ground beef heart and beef kidney, mixed with beef suet, browned minced onions, and sanguined spices. Which spices? Cumin and chili powder and something else. Something magical. Nobody knows what but the coney chefs, and if they told then they would not be gods.

The truth is, they may not have realized at first the specialness of what they had created. These Greeks, these Macedonians, these Albanians and Ruthenians and Rumanians had arrived in factory towns to take up jobs in the factories and to serve the factory workers. The immigrants hemmed trousers, cobbled shoes, thatched nobs. They sold their coneys on the side to earn a little extra, but soon they noticed that the coneys brought in more gold than their trades.

It was filling food; as heavy as it was delicious. The X Automobilians, whether sweating in the foundries, grinding through midnight shifts at the metal center, or straining over dies and tools with bright lights for hours, could fill up in five minutes with a coney and coffee. It was the perfect food for an assembly line town, as demonstrated by the ordering shorthand that sprang into life like a new language: "One up" meant a coney with everything; a milestone of verbal economy and the inverse relationship of calories to syllables. So coney stands became Coney Island restaurants. They bloomed fruitful and fecund, increased in number. Multiplied across the earth and increased upon it.

By the mid-twenties some three dozen Coney Islands in Akawe served up tens of thousands of coneys a day built by hundreds of restaurant employees. Balkan assembly line workers bent over their stations for hours: one man grilled the Goerlich's, another steered it to its bun and plate, where the next station provided the dressing, nothing written down, everything achieved with hands and voice, as demanding of speed and rigor as riveting.

I'm not exaggerating when I tell you that there were so many Coney Islands that they were served over the river water; two restaurants opened on the midst of the East Street Bridge and stayed there for decades. I'm not exaggerating when I tell you that the Coney Islands were open 24-7-365. Once, during a flood, a Coney had to close up, and hire a security guard to watch the door because the owners had lost the keys years earlier.

The Coney Islands thrived along the factory zones. They pulsed along Akawe's main arteries. They anchored each neighborhood and kept their street corners noisy all night long, from the wail of the evening whistle to the chiming of the church bells.

When the factories started to wither, the Coney Islands did too.

They held on longer than the factory jobs but, one by one, the great restaurants closed their doors. Midnight Oil Coney Island, Akawe Old Fashioned Coney Island, Delicious Coneys, Joe's Original Coney Island, and most of the others dried up through the 80s. By 1993, there were less than a dozen left.

The most famous Coney Island in Akawe, and possibly the world, is King Carol's, which presides over the Os like a tired king over a motley court of derelicts. It's okay, I guess, but it isn't my favorite. We had two on the South Side, both on Whitmore Road; the Kaleidoscope and the Constellation. The Kaleidoscope was closer to home and Radcliffe, but the waitresses weren't very nice there. I liked the Constellation more, with a blazing marquee featuring Orion shooting an arrow at the Great Bear. On the inside, sauced with color, supershined wood-veneer Formica tables stood sturdy under bright green hanging plants. Waitresses, young and old, but mostly old, bustled back and forth with steaming metal carafes of coffee, while the owner, an aging Albanian, banged on a small bell whenever an order appeared in his window.

The rippled glass lamps waved out a warm, amber light.

It seemed to drive away the winter.

www.ingramcontent.com/pod-product-compliance
Lightning Source LLC
Chambersburg PA
CBHW071404170626
46811CB00003B/1255